Broken Promises

By Chrissie Loveday.

End Of A Dream

CAROLYN sat in the taxi with her brother, on their way to her wedding. She could hardly speak for the excitement of it all. This was the happiest day of her life and the day she had been waiting for... for ever, it seemed.

"Nearly there, love," Paul said. "Half an hour or so and you'll be Mrs Henry Jacobs."

Carolyn smiled and took his hand.

"Thanks for being here for me. Mum and Dad would have loved to see this day, wouldn't they?"

"I'm proud to be here. And yes. Mum and Dad would have been as proud as I am. Even prouder if that's possible."

Carolyn's wedding dress was a simple strapless gown that showed off her figure perfectly. It was a short dress, and she was wearing a tiny veil. Her long hair was done up on top with little curls falling down either side of her face.

"Here we go. Wish me luck."

Paul grinned at his sister and held her hand.

The taxi drew up outside the church and a photographer appeared as if by magic.

"Smile, please. I'd like a shot of you getting out if you can do it elegantly. Help her, will you... Paul, isn't it?"

Paul nodded.

"That's right." The photographer smiled at Carolyn. "Straighten your veil."

"Is he here? Henry, I mean," she asked.

"I'm not sure," the photographer replied. "I'm detailed to get pictures of you."

"Of course he will be," Paul said firmly and she smiled at him as he helped her out of the car and took her arm, ready to walk her down the aisle.

In the porch, her chief bridesmaid was looking concerned.

"Nothing to worry about, love," she tried to reassure Carolyn, "but Henry seems to have gone missing. He'll be back any moment, I'm sure. He was here before and just seems to have disappeared. Shall I go and check?" she asked Paul.

"Might look better if I go," Paul said. "Stay there a mo. I won't be long."

The next few minutes seemed like an eternity. Carolyn sensed there was something seriously wrong… She began to shiver in her light wedding dress. Suddenly, she tossed back her veil, handed her bouquet to her bridesmaid, opened the church door and marched down the aisle. The congregation started murmuring to each other and one or two of them rose from their seats, trying to intercept her. She brushed them aside, stopping at the altar.

"Where is he? Henry, I mean?" she demanded to one of the groomsmen.

And where was his best man, Jerry?

"Well, I'm not sure. He went out about five minutes ago. Jerry followed him."

"Could you please go and see what his problem is?"

"I think Paul went out after them." The groomsman was clearly upset and didn't quite know what to say.

Carolyn marched through to the vestry, where the vicar was standing, looking helplessly at the rear door.

"What's going on?"

"I don't really know. Your groom, Henry, disappeared through that door. His best man followed him and then your brother."

She glared at the poor man and charged out of the door just in time to see Henry disappearing along the road, driving a car she didn't even recognise.

"Henry?" she called in a pitifully broken voice. "Paul! What's going on?"

"It seems Henry has absconded. I didn't hear exactly what he said but he's gone."

"So the wedding's off?" she asked.

"I'm sorry but it looks like it."

"But why? Did he give a reason?"

"He simply said, 'It's no good. I can't do this to her.' I'm so sorry. What do you want to do?"

"After I've caught him and killed him, you mean? I don't know. I really can't believe it. I mean, why? What have I done to deserve this?" She was shaking with cold and anger.

"Here, borrow my coat." Paul hung it round her shoulders and she nodded her thanks. "I suppose we'd better go back inside and tell everyone."

"What about the reception?"

"I don't know. Shall I tell them to go ahead with it?"

"Why not? The food has all been paid for. I think the drink is on sale or return so maybe they can pay for that."

Paul stared at his sister. Since when had she become so practical?

"OK, I'll go and tell them. What are you going to do?"

"I think I'll go back to the flat – see if I can find Henry and ask him what he's playing at. Here, you'd better have your jacket back. I'll sneak out through here. I don't want to see anyone."

"Why don't you wait for me? I'll tell everyone to go to the reception and then I'll come back with you."

"No. You go with them. Someone will have to sort it all out. I'll be fine."

She rushed out of the rear door of the church to the waiting bridal car. The driver was somewhat bemused but did as she told him and dropped her back at the flat he'd collected her from less than an hour ago.

She thanked him, leaped out of the car, and ran up the stairs to the flat she'd shared with Henry for the past several years.

"Henry? Henry?" she called. "Are you here?"

Carolyn looked round the flat she'd left with such high hopes only an hour ago. Her clothes lay on the bed where she'd left them.

Sadly, she stripped off her wedding dress and changed back into jeans and jumper. She looked in the wardrobe and saw that everything that was Henry's had gone. He must have come straight here from the church and removed all his clothes.

"You swine," she muttered.

Then she sat down and cried as though her heart would break. She thought of the reception and all their friends eating their carefully selected menu. What a disaster. A total disaster. How could anyone do this to someone he claimed to love? She collapsed on the bed, sobbing, till she finally fell into an exhausted sleep.

She woke up to the sound of knocking but decided to ignore it. She didn't want to speak to anyone. She could hear someone calling her name.

"Carolyn. Carolyn, please answer me. Come on." It was Paul.

Slowly, she rose from the bed and went to open the door.

"Thank you. At last. You look a wreck," he said frankly.

"Thanks a lot. What do you want?"

"To make sure my little sister is all right."

"I'm just fine. Hunky-dory. Now will you please go?"

"No way. I shall stay here till I'm certain you're all right. Now, what is there to eat?"

She thought for a minute.

"There's nothing in. The fridge is turned off. Remember, we were going away on honeymoon. I emptied the lot and cleared out everything."

"No tins or anything like that?"

"Maybe some soup. But I don't want anything. Did people go to the reception?"

"A few of them. Nobody was very

enthusiastic – except Uncle Sydney. He was ready to eat for Britain. Even took a load of stuff away with him. The caterers were pretty decent. They said they wouldn't charge for some of the stuff, they'd take it back and freeze it. Save you some money."

"That's up to Henry. He can pay."

"Yes, about Henry…"

"What? Have you seen him?"

"No. Assuming he's ever found again of course, he may pay up." Paul didn't look convinced.

"What do you mean? Come on. What do you know?"

"Apparently, there were two rough-looking types who turned up at the church. They met him outside and spoke to him. I don't know exactly what was said but someone else said they'd overheard what sounded like threats being made."

"Threats? What sort of threats?"

"I'm only repeating sketchy comments. Something about taking it out on you. Must admit, it sounded strange. Can you think of any explanation?"

"None at all. I really don't understand. You mean they were threatening me? But why?"

"Maybe they were getting at Henry through you. I don't know."

"That's ridiculous. I don't understand any

of it. What's he supposed to have done, anyway?"

She frowned, desperately trying to think of anything he might have been involved in. As far as she knew, he'd got a job working in an office with computers. She didn't really know what he did with his days but it all seemed quite normal. She worked for a company specialising in interior home design, again something quite innocent.

Paul contemplated his sister. She was in no state to be left alone.

"Carolyn, I don't think you should stay here. Why don't you come home with me? Stay for as long as you like. It'll mean you won't be on your own and when Henry comes back to earth, he'll know where you are. Leave a note here and let him come back when he's ready."

"Oh, Paul, be sensible. Henry's gone. He's out of my life. I don't even pretend to understand why but his things have all been removed from the wardrobe and..." Tears filled her eyes and she began to sob again.

"Come on. Pack a few things and let's go."

"I've already packed, for the honeymoon. Where's my suitcase?" Then she remembered. Henry had it in his car.

"Henry had it in his boot," she told her brother. "Do you know where his car is?"

"Maybe it's down in the car park but I doubt it. He'd have needed it to take his stuff away. Has he left your luggage somewhere?"

"I don't know. Maybe it's in the bedroom."

She went into their bedroom and sitting on the floor beside the bed was her suitcase. He must have brought it back when he collected his stuff.

She opened it and tears immediately pricked her eyes. The stuff she'd packed for their honeymoon abroad would be no use here in England. She snapped it shut again and stuffed some jeans and a couple of tops into an overnight bag. That would do for now.

"Good girl. Come on. I'll stop and buy some food on our way. Mel will be away for a few more days so it will just be the two of us. She was gutted to miss your big day but it seems she hasn't missed anything after all."

Mel was his long-term girlfriend who was a steward on an airline.

"I wonder if he'll have cancelled the honeymoon? Flights and everything. I can't believe he's done this... We were supposed to be staying at a hotel near the airport. Should I phone them, do you think?"

"I'll give them a call." Paul asked for the

number and dialled it on his mobile.

"Hello? I'm calling on behalf of Henry Jacobs. Sorry? Oh, I see. He's already called? OK. Thanks." He turned to Carolyn.

"Seems he's beaten you to it. I bet he's also called the airport and the honeymoon hotel."

"If not, he can pay for the lot," Carolyn snapped. "Come on, then. Let's go."

She couldn't bear to be in this place any longer. Too many memories. She hadn't expected to see it again until after the honeymoon with her beloved Henry. Tears were streaming down her face but she didn't care. She followed her brother out to his car, dumped her bag into the rear seat and got in.

"Come on, love. Wipe your eyes and blow your nose."

"You sound like our parents," she said, almost laughing. "But you're quite right – time I gave up crying. Henry can go to... well, you know where."

"Good girl. What do you fancy for supper? I'll go and buy something now." He drew into the car park of the supermarket and stopped near the door.

"Anything you like," she muttered.

She sat staring round, still trying to make sense of all that had happened. She and Henry should have been enjoying everyone's company at their reception. Then they were going to drive to Heathrow and their hotel for the night.

"I will not cry again," she told herself, gritting her teeth.

Moments later, Paul arrived clutching a carrier bag full of shopping. He also had a large box of tissues which he handed to her.

"Just in case," he said with a grin.

He drove the short distance to his delightful cottage at the edge of the town. As they entered the cosy lounge, she gave her brother a wan smile.

"Thanks, Paul. It's good of you to put up with me."

"No worries, sis. Now, you make yourself at home. Dump your stuff in the spare bedroom while I go and sort out supper. I've got a couple of steaks and some salad."

"Sounds lovely," she said, though the thought of eating anything revolted her.

She went upstairs to the pretty bedroom, took out her jeans and tops and put them away in the drawers. She knew Mel must have organised the room as it was quite feminine looking.

She slumped down on the bed and glanced at her watch. It was almost eight o'clock.

"Oh, Henry, where are you? Why have you done this to me? To us?" she muttered. She swallowed hard, determined not to start crying again.

She went into the bathroom and saw her face in the mirror. She looked awful. Her eyes were red and swollen and mascara had run in rivulets down her cheeks.

She picked up a flannel and began to scrub at her face, unpinned her hair and allowed it to fall down into its normal style, then went downstairs.

Paul was busy at the cooker.

"I've poured you a glass of red. Drink it while the steaks are cooking."

"Thanks, Paul. I'm sorry I'm such a wet weekend," she apologised. "I promise I'll soon be better."

"I'm sure you will."

Sorrow And Regrets

HENRY had been on the run for the past 24 hours. He had collected his things from their flat and tossed them all into the back of his car.

He hated doing this to her. Carolyn did not deserve it but if he had stayed and gone through with the wedding, he dreaded what might happen to her.

What had those men said? He needed to pay them or they'd take it out on Carolyn. He really loved her and knew he'd probably broken her heart. He was so ashamed of things he'd done at work and knew he'd been stupid. He had never told anyone about the massive fraud he'd become involved in and it was only when he'd realised all the implications, he'd pulled out.

The two heavies were sent by the man who had started him on this road to nowhere. He was not happy at all and made sure that he, Henry, knew exactly how he felt.

Henry really hoped that he was now safe and that Carolyn would be able to forgive him. Who could tell, one day perhaps they might get together again.

It had all begun when Henry had met the man he came to call Boss Man, one evening after work. He'd been for a drink with several colleagues and they had all gone home. He finished his drink and was about to leave the pub when Boss Man came and sat beside him, handing him another glass of wine.

"Henry, isn't it?"

"Do I know you?"

"Not yet, you don't. I'm hoping to put that right very soon. You work for Phoenix, don't you?"

"Well, yes."

"I have a proposition to put to you. Make us both a lot of money. And I mean a lot. More than you could ever dream of making. You're getting married soon, aren't you? I know all about you. About Carolyn, too."

"I don't know how you've found out all this. But forget it, I'm not interested."

"Don't rush away. I know you'd like a few hundred thousand to add to your bank account. Buy a nice place to live for the lovely Carolyn. Nobody loses out, I promise you – only Phoenix, and they can well afford it. I just need some information from you. Just a few amendments to your company's profile."

"I'm sorry. You've picked the wrong guy for this job. Now, if you'll excuse me."

Henry tried to rise but the man stopped him.

"You really don't mean that, Henry. I know you'll be willing to help. There will be consequences for both of you if you don't."

"You sound threatening. I don't like that."

"I'm sorry. But I really want you to work for me. Just a few alterations here and there."

"How do you mean, alterations?"

"Good. You're getting interested. You're a smart man. That's why I chose you. It's all quite simple."

He launched into a description of Henry's job and how he could help. It really did sound very easy and he was going to be paid a lot of money. It would mean they could buy a really nice flat or even a house. Boss Man explained what he needed to be done and how it might change things.

"You do make it sound quite easy," Henry admitted. "How would I get the money?"

"I'll organise payment so that it can't be traced. Just leave that to me."

Henry asked for time to think about it and Boss Man agreed. He suggested meeting the following evening and they parted.

Looking back, Henry knew he should never have agreed to the man's proposal. It really hadn't sounded a big deal until he'd come to try it. Once he'd made a start, he suddenly realised the deep significance of it all and called it off.

He felt incredibly guilty about even attempting the scam and prayed that there was no trace left of his aborted intervention. The only problem he had was how to tell the Boss Man.

When Henry didn't turn up for the meeting with the Boss Man, two heavies came to see him. He had desperately tried to explain to them that it was impossible to do what their boss wanted and they had turned very nasty. It was all just before the wedding... they had told him that they would seriously harm Carolyn, if not actually kill her.

Feeling desperate, Henry had almost told Carolyn about it all but didn't really want to admit to his stupidity. He was getting more and more scared... in fact terrified described his feelings more accurately. When he saw them waiting at the back of the church, he'd decided to run for it. They made sure he'd seen they were carrying guns and suddenly he realised they meant everything they said.

Only for Carolyn's sake, he decided she was safer without him. He'd almost contacted his fiancée several times since leaving her but, fearing for her safety, had left it. It was something he needed to do before too long. Nobody could keep searching for him for ever, surely.

But how could Carolyn ever forgive him? He knew she'd never understand. She was much too honest.

On reflection, he didn't know why he'd even been tempted to commit this fraud. He sat in his car, thinking about the events of the past few weeks, culminating in the abandoned wedding.

Tears filled his eyes. They should have been in the Seychelles, enjoying its wonders. Instead, he was living amongst all the rubbish of his life, packed into a car.

He looked out at the Cornish scenery. It meant nothing to him. Hills and valleys, streams and flowers. He could barely see them. What on earth was he going to do next? He'd driven here in desperation after leaving their home. It was far enough away to give him time to think.

Everyone at his office had expected him to be away on honeymoon for two weeks so he knew he'd be safe for a while. He'd actually done nothing wrong. Maybe he should come clean and tell the heads of the company and if they fired him, so be it. He deserved it.

For the umpteenth time, he'd thought of going back and then changed his mind. He didn't want Carolyn to suffer. He shuddered at the very thought.

He'd turned his mobile off and so had remained unaware of the one call she had made to him. Scared of being tracked, he'd decided to leave it switched off. He knew the Boss Man had his number. He didn't know how he'd obtained it but he had and was probably capable of tracking him. He was clearly a powerful man with a lot of paid muscle behind him.

He sat there, wondering what on earth to do next. His money would run out quite soon. He didn't even want to draw any cash or use his credit cards in case of being followed.

"Oh, Carolyn," he murmured. "I'm so sorry. Can you ever forgive me?"

****

After staying with her brother for a couple of days, Carolyn felt it was time to return to the flat. His girlfriend Mel was due back home again and she didn't want to be in their way.

"I think I should go home, Paul. You've been wonderful but I need to get used to the single life again. I'll be fine now."

"I don't think you should go just yet. I mean to say, what will you do all day?"

"I could always go back to work."

"It's much too soon. They'll all want to ask you questions and could you cope with everyone feeling sorry for you? Stay here a bit longer."

"You need your space back. And you need to go back to work. They won't be happy with you if you take more time off. I'll go back this afternoon. Don't try to persuade me otherwise, please."

Paul gave a shrug. He knew better than to try to persuade his sister to do something against her will.

"Well, if you think you're ready. But promise me you'll phone me every day, morning and evening. I need to know you're OK."

She agreed and began to pack up her things.

"I'll run you back," he offered. "Your car is still at the flat?" She nodded. "I'll make us some lunch and then we'll go to your place. You'll need some shopping too."

"How on earth did you get to be so organised and practical?" she asked him.

"Comes naturally, of course." He laughed. "I'll go and see what there is to eat."

He produced a quick lunch of bread and cheese and some salad. She couldn't help but smile at him.

"Thanks so much for looking after me. You've been amazing. And I do admire your housekeeping. Mum would have been proud of you."

"Aw, shucks," he replied, adopting a dreadful American twang. "Ya shouldn't flatter me so."

She smiled at him and clutched his hand, feeling her tears starting to flow again.

"Hey, come on." He gave her a hug. "Are you really sure you want to go home?"

"Yes, of course. It's just when people are nice to me... I think I'll go back to work in a couple of days. That'll keep my mind occupied."

"But people might just be too nice to you. If you cry every time that happens..."

"I'll be fine. Give me a couple of days and I'll cope with anything. When do you expect Mel back?"

"Not sure. Probably not till later tonight. So I'll have plenty of time to install you back at your place and do some food shopping on our way."

They stood in the supermarket. Paul was trying to encourage her to think about meals and what she might need, but she had no heart in it and stared blankly at the shelves.

In desperation, Paul shoved several tins and things for the freezer into the trolley. He added fresh fruit and vegetables and continued to the checkout.

"Oh, have you got tea and coffee at home?"

"I don't know. Probably," she muttered.

"I'll pick some up. And milk and bread. You must have stuff to spread on it."

"Probably."

"Come on, Carolyn. Face up to it. You're on your own again and you need to get your life back on track. Or come back with me and stay with us."

"I'm so sorry. You're right, of course. I need to get myself together. Right. I'll have marmalade and cheese. I can make cheese on toast for supper."

"No, you won't. You'll cook something sensible. I've put a fish pie in the trolley. You should have that."

"You always did like to boss me around, didn't you?"

"You need looking after. Who else will do it if I don't?"

She paid with her credit card and they drove back to her flat. It really was hers now. She'd bought it with money left to her by her parents and Henry had moved in with her. This was about to be the first time she'd ever lived there on her own.

It would be very strange not waiting for him to come in from work. Often she was home first and usually put some dinner together ready for when he came in.

Now it was a single meal and she could eat whenever she wanted to.

She hated the whole idea.

****

Paul went inside first. There several letters on the mat and she glanced at them.

"I can't read them now."

He carried the shopping into the kitchen and put it all away in the fridge and freezer. His sister was sitting in the main room, looking miserable. He was reaching the end of his tether with her but maintained his patience a while longer.

He went into their bedroom and saw the wedding dress dumped on the floor. He picked it up, remembering her excitement as they'd driven in the taxi to church.

"You rat, Henry," he murmured. "Why on earth did you do it?"

He picked the dress up, put it into the bag and stuffed it into the back of the wardrobe then took it out again, deciding to take it back to his place. Out of sight, out of mind, he thought.

He straightened the bed cover and went back into the lounge.

"Right. I've put the shopping away and put your bag on the bed. I'll leave you to unpack. You sure you'll be all right?"

"One day maybe," she replied enigmatically. "Yes. I'll be fine. You go back home now. Get ready for Mel's return. Don't worry about me. I'll work things out."

"OK, then. I'll be off. I'll call you later."

"Thanks. Thank you so much for everything. Especially thank you for being my brother. Everyone should have one."

He took her in his arms and gave her a big hug, wiping away the tears that were forming.

"I'm happy to be here for you. Let's face it, we've needed each other for a few years now. Since the parents left us, it's been down to us to stay together."

"You do more for me than I do for you. I'm sorry."

"Hey, you're my kid sister. You'd barely finished university when they went. You've come a long way since then."

The dreadful car accident had devastated both of them at the time. Their parents had been travelling along a motorway when a lorry had lost control and had crushed their car. They had both been killed instantly.

Paul and Carolyn had stood side by side at their funeral, lost and wondering how on earth they'd ever cope. It had all happened over five years ago and they had done their best to come to terms with it all and moved on. At least their parents had left them enough money to buy their own places to live and some left over.

"You're right. We've had worse things to cope with than this. I suppose I'll come to terms with the loss of Henry. It's all just a bit raw at the moment."

"I know you'll be all right. I'll call you later. 'Bye now."

"'Bye, and thanks again."

Carolyn forced herself to go into the bedroom. She had expected to see her discarded wedding dress lying on the floor. She rushed to the wardrobe and saw it had gone. Paul must have taken it.

Perhaps it was just as well. She wasn't really sure she wanted to see it ever again.

Sadly, she unpacked the bag she'd taken to Paul's and looked at her honeymoon case. Taking a deep breath, she opened it and began to take out all her lovely things. She laid them all on the bed, trying to decide where she would put them. She had plenty of storage space, especially now that Henry's stuff had gone.

Wiping away the tears that seemed to have filled her eyes yet again, she drew in another deep breath and went through to the kitchen where she put on the kettle to make herself some coffee. She would get over this. She was determined.

Life Goes On

IT was a month since the day that Henry had let her down. Carolyn tried to hate him but she couldn't. Ever since her return home, she found herself making excuses for his behaviour. She hadn't even mentioned his name to her work colleagues after she had returned to work. Everyone treated her differently and they all seemed to want to sympathise. She had finally stood up in the middle of the office and made a speech.

"I know you're all sorry for me and want to help me. Henry's gone, I don't know where, but it would really help me if you treated me normally and didn't look at me as if I'm about to burst into tears. I might cry sometimes but please, I beg you, just let me shed my tears and don't sympathise with me. Thank you all."

There had been a slight murmuring amongst her friends and then someone had started to clap. Soon they had all begun to join in and that was it. Since that moment, they'd been treating her just as they always had done and she managed to work properly and get on with her life.

Several of her girl friends had asked her to

join them for a drink after work and she'd even been to the theatre with some of them. Her words had had the effect she'd hoped for and she was beginning to think she was really starting a new life.

Paul had let her off calling him twice a day and was content with her occasional calls. He usually invited her to join them for a meal on Sundays but she declined, preferring to stay alone and cook something simple for herself. Mind you, she was getting sick of scrambled eggs and cheese on toast and planned to make more of an effort at some point in the future.

One Saturday, the phone rang and Paul invited her to come over for a barbecue.

"Get into your car and get yourself over here. We've got several friends coming round and they all know about your situation. They won't say a word."

"OK, thanks. What time?"

"Come now. You can help prepare the salads."

"On my way," she said with a smile.

She went to change into something reasonably suitable for a barbecue and set off, stopping at the supermarket on her way past and bought some wine. She looked at other stuff and decided her brother and his girlfriend would have everything organised.

When she reached the cottage, she wondered where she should park. There were several cars parked outside their garden and so she parked some way along the road. As she walked to the door, she wondered who would be there. She knew many of Paul's friends. She brushed a stray hair out of her eyes and knocked at the door.

"Hi, there," Paul said cheerfully. "Come on in. Everyone's come early so the party's started."

"I brought some wine," she told him. "And I'm sorry but I left it in the car."

"No worries. There's plenty here. We can always get it when we've run out."

"Sorry," she said. "Don't know what I was thinking."

"Carolyn. Lovely to see you," Mel said, running from the kitchen to give her a hug. "You're just in time to give me a hand with some of the salads, if you don't mind."

"Of course not. Gives me a purpose in life."

"Now that sounds sad. Come on. Paul is busy with the fire and that seems to take all his time. Typical male, isn't he?"

Carolyn smiled and followed her to the kitchen. Soon they were carrying out large bowls of salad and she had to face the crowd.

"Carolyn. You're looking super." She was embraced by Jack, an old friend of her brother's. "I think you know Katie and then there's Dave and Tracey."

"Hi, everyone. Good to see you again," she said, not even knowing who a couple of them were. But it didn't seem to matter. They welcomed her into the group and soon she was sitting with a glass of wine in her hand and she forgot she was single for a little while.

Paul went inside and came back with a man she hadn't seen before.

"This is Jed, a friend of mine," Paul introduced him to the others. "Make him welcome, please. There's a space next to my sister, Carolyn. Shove up, sis, and make some space. I'll get you some wine, Jed."

"Sorry, I didn't mean to bump into you like that," Jed said to Carolyn.

"No worries. Sorry I didn't make more room for you. Are you OK there?"

"Yes. Thanks, Paul," he said as he was handed some wine.

"Can I top you up?" Paul asked his sister.

"I mustn't drink too much or I won't be able to drive home," she told her brother.

"You can always stay over. Come on. Drink up."

She accepted a refill and sat back, ready to enjoy herself. Jed seemed nice. He was certainly a good-looking bloke and easy company. She wondered why she'd never met him before and why Paul had never mentioned him.

"So, how do you know Paul?"

"We used to play rugger together for a time. Then I moved to Cornwall and we sort of lost touch. I was coming to see my parents and wanted to see him. Here I am."

"I see. What do you do?"

"I'm a freelance photographer. Local papers, magazines and so on. Makes me a living and I adore living in Cornwall. It's so lovely. Do you know it?"

"Not really. Well, I think I might know around the St Ives area. We went there for a holiday when I was small. I think Paul and Mel have been back a few times."

"You should come and visit again."

"I'll think about it. I take it you're not married?"

"Me? No. Think I'm allergic the whole idea of marriage. How about you?"

Carolyn gulped. She'd assumed they all knew about her disastrous wedding day.

"No, I'm not married," she managed to say without shedding a tear.

"Not attached in any way?"

"No. No attachments." She couldn't help but feel guilty as she said this but she stuck to it and didn't even blush.

"Here we go," Paul said as he placed a large platter full of cooked meat on the table. Everyone complimented him and reached out to fill their plates.

"There's cutlery in the middle and Mel, can you put the salads on the table? It'll be easier if everyone stays where they are."

Mel carried several bowls over and put them on to the large table.

It actually felt good, Carolyn realised, to be sitting out in their cottage garden with friends. She smiled at Paul and winked at him. He smiled back at her and filled his own plate.

"Here's to the cooks," Jack said, raising his glass.

When all the food had been eaten and everyone vowed they'd never eat again, they cleared the empty dishes away and the girls all went into the kitchen to wash up, despite Mel's protestations.

"You don't have to do this. Really. I'll do it with Paul later."

"We're doing it and that's that," Tracey insisted. "Besides, it gives us a chance to catch up with the gossip."

Carolyn felt herself blushing and felt suddenly weak. She made some excuse to go upstairs and when she came back, they'd all more or less finished.

"You all right, love?" Mel asked kindly.

Carolyn nodded.

"Don't worry," Mel assured her, reading her thoughts, "they didn't mention you at all. I take it you haven't heard anything of Henry?"

"Not a thing. I'm not even thinking of him any more. I just get mad when I do."

"Good for you. Jed's nice, don't you think?"

"I suppose he is. I hadn't really thought about it. He lives in Cornwall anyway, so he isn't much use as a potential long term relationship," she joked.

"Shame you didn't get to know him before he went off to live in the wilds." Mel laughed. "Now, let's get another drink. You are staying, I presume?"

"Well, thanks. If I have another drink, I may need to."

The evening wore on and they all moved inside the small lounge as it got cooler. Jed sat close by Carolyn for most of the time and seemed to enjoy her company. She felt guilty but gradually relaxed, until she felt his arm slide across the back of her. She stiffened and wondered how to tell him to stop it.

Then his hand started to move across her neck. She moved away.

"Sorry, I'm not ready for this yet," she said and ran upstairs. Paul followed her and spoke to her gently.

"Come on, love. Jed was only being friendly. Don't condemn him. He's had a bad time, too, and was probably only seeking a bit of comfort."

"I'm sorry. It was just a bit of a shock."

"Come back downstairs. He won't try it again, I'm sure."

She followed him down again and went to sit next to Jed. He smiled at her and mumbled, "Sorry."

Carolyn explained she was just a bit sensitive at the moment and apologised herself.

Some of the group decided to call it a day and went off home, leaving only Carolyn and Jed with Paul and Mel. They talked for a while until Carolyn said she was almost falling asleep and must go to bed.

"Will you be all right on the sofa, Jed? It's reasonably long so you won't be too cramped."

"I'll be fine. It's very good of you to put me up at all."

"Purely selfish, of course. Gives us tomorrow to really talk again. Need to catch up on the past few years. Have we got a duvet or something for him, Mel?"

Mel went up to the spare room and came down with a duvet and pillow. She and Paul then went up to bed and left Jed and

Carolyn downstairs.

"You want to talk about it?" he asked.

"I'm not sure it would do any good. I was dumped at the altar. No warning. It takes a lot to get over that but I'm getting there."

"I lost my girlfriend. She went off with another man and left me alone. I went to Cornwall as a sort of escape. It was a couple of years ago. I've sort of made a life there now, and though I feel lonely at times, it's a good place to be."

"I'm sorry. Sorry, too, that I reacted the way I did. It was a shock, I suppose."

"It was thoughtless of me. But you're so lovely and, well, human nature..."

"Thanks for explaining, anyway. I really must go to bed now before I fall asleep where I stand." To her own surprise, she stood on tiptoe and kissed him lightly on his cheek. "Night-night."

He looked surprised and touched where she'd kissed him.

"Night," he whispered, watching her go upstairs.

Jed realised he felt very attracted to her. Her soft brown eyes held an expression of gentleness. He liked that. Could there be any future for him with Carolyn? He really didn't know but wanted to... well, to get to know her much more.

He settled down to sleep but it was a long

time coming, even though he'd driven all the way here in one go and should be tired after the journey. He was planning to stay for a few days at least and hoped he would get to see much more of his friend's sister.

* * * *

Carolyn fell asleep quite quickly but woke early. She was desperate for some tea but knew she couldn't go and make it without disturbing Jed. The stairs led down into the lounge where he was sleeping.

She lay there, reflecting on the previous evening. It had been fun and she had to admit to enjoying chatting to their friends. Nobody had said a word to her about Henry and that felt good.

She still missed him. She wondered where he was and why he had never got in touch with her. She longed for him to come into the flat with his usual cheery "Hi, there!"

Tears starting to prick at her eyes and blinked them away. She heard movement and sat up. Someone knocked at her door.

"Come in," she replied.

"Hope you don't mind. I made some tea and brought it up."

Jed looked ruffled and wearing only a singlet and shorts, really looked very attractive.

"You must be a mind-reader. I was wondering if I might creep past you to make some. Here, sit down on the bed." She took the mug from him and he sat beside her.

"I think Mel and Paul are both still in dreamland. No sounds from them anyway. So, how did you sleep?"

"Quite well, actually. You?"

"Not a lot. I was thinking about all the chaos that hit you. I really do feel for you."

"Thanks, but I'm not allowing myself to think about it any more. He's gone. Four years obviously meant less to him than it did to me, so that's that."

"Well said. You're very lovely and you certainly won't find it hard to find someone else."

"Well, thank you. But I'm not sure I'll ever want anyone else. After Henry, well... once bitten and all that..."

"Then I'll have to set about changing your views. How about coming out to lunch with me? It's OK, I'll invite Paul and Mel, too." He noticed her slight look of panic at his suggestion.

"I really ought to go back home. I only left for an evening," she protested.

"What do you have to do? I mean to say, have you left the cooker on or something? Left the fridge defrosting?"

She giggled.

"Nothing like that. I usually clean on Sundays. Do washing. That sort of thing."

He yawned loudly.

"Sorry, but that doesn't sound like a very pressing engagement." He grinned at her and slowly she smiled back.

"OK. Lunch it is, but we'll go Dutch, I insist."

"That won't work as I want to treat Paul and Mel," Jed told her. "You might as well just accept it."

"Persistent, aren't you? Thanks. I might have to go back to my flat to change, though."

"I suppose I should go and get dressed before Paul thinks I'm up to no good. I'd hate for your reputation to be damaged."

"Yes. It doesn't really look good to have you sitting on my bed half dressed – despite the provision of tea, of course. And for your future information, I don't usually drink it with milk."

"Most promising thing I've heard all morning. Suggests you might allow me to make tea for you again."

****

Jed left her to get up and dressed and went downstairs. He felt pleased with

Carolyn's reactions and hoped he would be seeing more of her during his stay. He realised it was all a bit soon for her but maybe, as long as he played his cards correctly, they might have a chance.

He would certainly be keen on that, but was determined not to hurry things. He could see that Carolyn was potentially all he could want in a woman. His problem was how to convince her of that in the short time he'd have available.

When she came downstairs, she found Jed sitting reading the paper.

"Do you want some breakfast?" she asked.

"Will they mind? I mean it isn't exactly our kitchen, is it?" Jed said hesitantly.

"Paul's my brother. He won't mind at all. Don't forget I stayed here for ages. Well, a couple of days, anyway." She laughed. "I'll make some toast and see what there is to put on it. You stay there. You can tell me what's going on in the big wide world."

"I was looking at some of the pictures actually." He pointed at the photographs accompanying the main newspaper stories. "One or two really good ones, but several of them are far and away from decent. I'd love to have a job where I could really show them. Frustrating in the extreme."

"How good are you? If you don't rate

these pictures, I mean to say..."

"Oh, I suppose I'm not brilliant. It's frustration talking. Some of the angles are pretty suspect and I think there's more of a story there somewhere. Forget it. It's just me sounding off."

She shrugged and went in search of bread to make toast. She put four slices of bread into the toaster and put the kettle on.

"More tea?" she called to him.

"Please. I'll come through."

"It's all right. There's not exactly a lot of space in here."

"Sounds good to me."

Carolyn gave a shiver. He was certainly making no bones about fancying her. She felt embarrassed. It was only a short time since she was abandoned at the altar and there was no way she should even be looking at anyone else.

"Jed," she began. "Jed, I'm a bit..." she was going to say vulnerable or delicate but somehow she stopped.

"Look, you've told me about Henry and what you went through, so no worries there. Trouble is, I really like you and I'm only here for a short time. I did meet you before. I was at one of Paul's parties and you were there with Henry. Ages ago. I fancied you then, but you only had eyes for him."

"Really? I don't remember that."

"It was new love for you, I remember, and you seemed to see nobody else. I was also with my lady so maybe you wouldn't have noticed."

"How could you fancy me when you were with someone else?"

"Sorry. Doesn't sound very flattering, does it? It was starting to go a bit sour even then."

"One could hardly miss you now. Maybe you've grown some since then!"

Her reference to his being just over six feet in height made him smile.

"Watch out, the toast is about to burst into flames," he said, reaching round her to press the button. He brushed her bare arms as he did so and Carolyn felt a strange sort of tremor run through her. It was ridiculous. She hardly knew him and put it down to her vulnerable state. She was, after all, feeling rather sensitive.

Was she ready for the attentions of another man? She gave a shiver. What nonsense, she thought. She was no more ready to embark on anything new than fly to the moon.

"I think it's still edible, just about." He pointed to the toast.

"Sorry, I wasn't thinking. I'm not good in the kitchen. But then, I'm not the most practical person when let loose in any kitchen. Henry was always complaining about my lack of ability."

"Then Henry was rather silly. I think you look lovely with Mel's apron round you and it was just because I was talking to you that the toast nearly burned. Have you found anything to spread on it?" he asked.

"In the cupboard over the sink."

He reached into the cupboard and produced a range of jams and marmalade and also a pot of honey. She put out two plates for the toast.

Absentmindedly, she spread butter on all the toast and started to add marmalade.

"Whoa there. I don't like marmalade," Jed told her. "Jam or honey for me."

"Sorry. I wasn't thinking."

"Strikes me you were thinking a bit too much. Here. Give me my plate. I'll do the rest. You go and sit down and I'll bring the tea in to you."

"Thanks," she said. "I think maybe I'm not properly awake yet."

A Proposal To Consider

THE two of them seemed to find plenty to talk about. They went to sit out in the small garden and enjoyed the summer sunshine. It was well after eleven o'clock before Paul and Mel came down.

"Hello, you two. Hope you found some breakfast. Sorry we're so late," Mel apologised. "Only just woke up. My last day of rest before I go back to work in the morning. Well, later tonight, actually."

Mel's job as an air steward gave her rather erratic hours and often she had to leave home in the middle of the night.

"Where are you going this time?" Carolyn asked.

"Long haul to Australia," Mel replied. "I'll be away for a week or so."

"However do you cope, Paul?" Jed asked.

"Oh, it gives me space to enjoy life," he teased.

"Watch it, you!" Mel returned. "I'll leave you a list of things to do while I'm away."

"Don't worry. I've got heaps to do. Looking after this character for one thing. You're staying till next weekend, aren't you, Jed?"

44

"I hope so. I'd quite like to do a bit of work around here. Some moody shots of life in a city."

"Hardly a city. It's pretty enough, though. I'll take you round some of the sights."

"Don't forget I lived here – I do know my way around."

"Yes, of course. Sorry. I've got a couple of days off anyway, so maybe we can do something then," Paul suggested.

"Great. What are you doing, Carolyn?" Jed asked.

"Working, of course."

"Can't you get some time off, too? Be good to all go out together."

"I don't know. Maybe later in the week."

"I'm off tomorrow and Tuesday," Paul told her. "Could you get time off then?"

"I'm not like you, I can't just get time off whenever I want it. I can maybe get Thursday off. Not before then, though."

"That's a date." Jed smiled. "Now, you two, are you ready to go out for lunch? On me, of course."

"There's no need for that."

"I want to. Least I can do. I'm going to take Carolyn home to get changed and we'll come back to pick you up."

"I can drive myself," Carolyn said. "I've got my car parked down the road. I'll go and change and meet you there... where are we going?"

"I insist on driving you."

"I'm perfectly able to drive myself, thank you," she said, adamant.

"Then I shall come and collect you when you're ready. Go on, shoo. Get glammed up ready for the meal of your life."

She giggled, went upstairs to collect her jacket and handbag, said her goodbyes and set off along the road to where she had left her car.

She paused. She could have sworn she'd left it along here but there was no sign of it. She turned and went the other way but it had gone. Disappeared! Who on earth would want to steal it? It was hardly a new model and a rather boring one anyway, she thought.

She went back into Paul's place.

"My car. It's gone. It must have been stolen."

"No! How awful. Where did you leave it?"

"Quite a bit along the road. I just stopped in the first available space. Oh, heavens, what should I do?"

"I'll call the police," Paul said firmly. "Don't worry, love, possibly they've found it already. Joy riders, I expect." He went back inside and called the police.

"I'll take you home, if you really need to go and change," Jed offered. "But you'll do fine as you are."

"I can't even contemplate going out for lunch," Carolyn protested. "Sorry – but I need to get this sorted first. What on earth shall I do if they haven't found it?"

They were all sympathetic and made various suggestions, including Jed offering to take and fetch her from work. She explained that she needed her car to go and visit clients and that she might need to hire a car.

Paul returned and said the police would keep a look out for it and provided a report number.

"What on earth use is that?"

"So you can report it to your insurance company, idiot. Have you got your details with you?"

"I don't know."

"You're supposed to carry your insurance certificate whenever you drive the car. Don't tell me you've left it in the car."

"No, I haven't. I've got the certificate but not the phone number."

Finally, they agreed to go to her flat and sort it out from there. They went in two cars so they were independent of each other. Jed led the way with Carolyn beside him.

"Don't worry too much, Carolyn. I'll be here to drive you wherever you need to go."

Carolyn smiled.

"Thanks, it's good of you. But it is your holiday and I don't want to spoil it."

"Being with you is holiday enough for me. I really like you, you know."

"So you said. But it's much too soon for me. I'm not over Henry yet."

"Who said you need to be? Surely we can be friends simply spending time together?"

"As long as that's all it is. Turn left here. There are usually plenty of parking spaces."

They parked outside the flat in the dedicated parking area. Upstairs in her flat, he looked round appreciatively.

"This is nice," he told her. "You've furnished it beautifully. Just right. Minimalist but still comfortable and homely."

"I should hope so." Caroline smiled. "It is my job, after all. Not that I get many places like this to design for. My clients are usually very wealthy and want gold trimmings on everything."

"Now that must be tough."

"Not really. I just pander to their wishes and then make suggestions about changing it. Now, I must look for my insurance stuff. Excuse me."

She went to her desk and started to look through her various files. She pulled out the documents she needed and found the number to call. She gave them the details and also the report number provided by the police.

"But what do I do in the meantime?" she asked. "I need my car for work."

She was told to wait for a day and see if it was found and if not, then to hire a similar-sized car.

"That's a fat lot of good," she said as she put the phone down. "Looks as though I'll have to take tomorrow off, after all."

"Excellent," Jed replied. "I think the others are here. Shall I let them in?"

They all discussed what should happen next and decided to go to the pub for lunch.

"The police have your mobile number so if they hear anything, they'll call you. So come on. Let's go and eat."

Somewhat unwillingly, Carolyn agreed to go. She still felt very worried about whether she'd get her car back in one piece.

They were eating dessert when her phone rang. It was the police to say they'd found a burned-out wreck of a car similar to hers. She went white and slumped back heavily.

"When will you know if it's mine?" She listened for a while. "It does sound like mine. Is there nothing left to identify it positively? I see. Well, thank you." She switched off her phone. "Looks as though I'm buying a new car."

"Oh, rotten luck. What's happened?" Mel asked.

She told them and they were sympathetic.

"I'll need to hire something while I look. Not sure if the insurance will pay for it or not."

"Leave it for a day or two and take up my offer," Jed suggested.

"I can't. Thanks a lot but I do need to be independent. I need to be able to manage on my own."

"I think you're being stupid, sis. Jed doesn't mind or he wouldn't offer. In fact I suspect he'd quite relish the idea of running you round."

"It's still too soon," she muttered. "I can't take up with someone else. Not yet – if ever."

"I'm only offering to drive you, not marry you," Jed protested, with a twinkle in his eye. "Not that I'd mind marrying you."

"How can I accept when you say things like that?"

Paul was laughing and so was Mel.

"Methinks the lady doth protest too much," Paul remarked.

"What? What do you mean by that remark?"

"Nothing, dear sister. Nothing at all. Stop being so prickly. Now, are we having coffee?"

Carolyn sat fuming. She felt none of them was taking her predicament seriously. She drank the coffee that someone had ordered and felt as if she was in the middle of a nightmare. Perhaps she would wake up any moment now and everything would be all right.

Her beloved little car should be there, parked in its usual place. But she knew it wasn't a dream. She would be forced to begin to search out a new car. This car held such sentimental value to her. She and Henry had bought it together about three years ago to celebrate her new promotion. She felt tears burning at her eyes.

"What do you think?" someone was asking her.

Carolyn gave a start.

"Sorry? Think about what?"

"We're thinking of taking a walk over the Downs Banks."

"Oh, you go if you want to. Leave me out of it."

"So what will you do instead? Sit and fret about your lack of car? Or maybe you'll sit and while away the afternoon crying again."

Paul clearly knew her all too well. What else would she do?

"All right. Downs Banks it is."

They all enjoyed their walk in the warm

sunshine and there was a lot of laughter and joking. Carolyn began to think there might indeed be a new life awaiting her. Jed even took her hand at one point and she didn't pull away.

That was certainly progress, she decided. It felt good to feel his touch, and it didn't actually commit her to anything, was it? They went back to her flat and she made tea.

"Sorry, I haven't got any food for you."

"Personally, I'm still full after lunch," Mel replied. "We should really be getting back, Paul. I've got to pack and I need to get some sleep. You stay on, Jed. In fact, I won't mind going on my own and you can take Paul back home."

"It's OK. I'll come with you," Paul said. "Can't have you going off without me and well, I'd like to be there for you. I'll give Jed my key so he can get back in whatever time he chooses. OK with you guys?"

"Fine by me," Jed told them. "As long as Carolyn won't mind putting up with me for a while longer."

"Well, no, I suppose not, though I do have some stuff to get ready for work tomorrow."

"I can maybe help. My skills aren't limited to photography, you realise. I can set things up to make a good impression."

"Oh, there's nothing like that. I just need to check my briefcase and sort out what I'm going to wear. General stuff like that. Won't take me long."

"And I'm going to be your chauffeur for the day."

"Well, you can take me to work. Thank you very much. If you're sure it won't put you out too much."

"You ready?" Paul asked Mel.

"I think so. Thanks for the tea, Carolyn. Nice to see you joining in with life again. I know it won't help you much but I have to say, I wasn't all that keen on Henry. Sorry, but I needed to say it."

"Well, you didn't have to live with him, did you?" Carolyn felt annoyed with Mel but didn't want to make a scene.

"Of course not. Sorry, I shouldn't have spoken. Take care, love. I'll say 'bye to you, too, Jed. I'm going around midnight so I doubt you'll even be awake then."

"'Bye, Mel, and thanks for putting me up. I'll see you next time. Have a good trip."

They left and Jed was left alone with Carolyn.

"Well, here we are. What would you like to do with what's left of today?" Jed asked.

"I haven't really thought about it. Anything you want to do?"

"To be honest, I usually slump in front of

television on Sunday evening. Calm before the storm of Monday morning."

"That's pretty much what I do, too. Do you mind if I go and change? I feel I've been living in this outfit." Caroline grinned ruefully.

"I don't mind at all. It's a very nice shirt, though. I'll always remember it with pleasure. Such a pretty blue. Makes your eyes look… well, I suppose they are brown but at times they look sort of dark blue. Bluey-brown-eyed blonde. Quite an unusual combination. My perfect woman."

"Nice of you to say so. You've got brown eyes, too. Quite a dark brown. The sort of brown someone could drown in… Sorry, I'm getting a bit carried away. Henry was quite blond. He probably still is."

"You haven't heard anything from him?"

"No, nothing. Sorry, I shouldn't be talking about him, to you of all people…"

"I don't mind. Tell me about it all and then I won't put my foot in it."

She began to fill him in on the details. She felt quite unemotional and for the first time, could speak about it in a quite matter-of-fact way.

"He was a bit odd just before it. The wedding, I mean. When I think about it, he was acting strangely during the week before. I reckon something must have happened. Something to upset him. But he left and as far as I'm concerned, I obviously meant little to him."

"I'm sorry. You don't deserve to be treated like that. I can't imagine what he thought he was doing."

"Believe me, neither can I. I've thought it through time and time again and still ended up with zero. But enough of me. Tell me about you."

"Not a lot to tell. I had a fiancée who decided she didn't want to know and left me for someone else. She's now happily married and expecting a baby. I went down to Cornwall to find work and a complete change of lifestyle. It really suits me down there."

He smiled.

"You should come down to visit. I bet it will catch you and fill your senses as it did me. It's such a wonderful place to live. Fresh air and gorgeous views. I'll show you some pictures. I'm assuming you haven't been again, not since you went when you were little?"

"I was very little. We did go that way once more. Might have been Devon, actually."

"It's quite different there. Still lovely, of course, just different. I do go to take pictures there sometimes. Always feel I'm going home when I return. I've got a cottage quite close to the sea. Well, I say next to the sea but it's some way above. It's got some amazing views, especially when the trees don't have leaves."

"You're quite a salesman. I'll certainly have to come and see it for myself."

"Good. When might that be?"

"Oh, I don't know. One day."

"How about coming back with me next week?"

"Next week? Oh, I couldn't possibly."

"Why not?"

She tried hard to think of reasons and fell back on her work load. Actually, it wasn't all that bad at the moment. She'd cleared most of her stuff before their aborted honeymoon and had been merely keeping up with things since then.

Besides, it was their quiet time of year when many folks were on holiday. A little holiday in Cornwall might be rather nice. But she couldn't possibly stay with Jed. She would see him every day but she certainly couldn't stay with him.

"Why not? I asked you that before you went into a sort of daze. I've got a spare room, so you'd be quite safe," he added with a grin.

"Let me think about it. And thank you. You're very kind. I'm not sure about staying with you, though. Spare room or no, I'm not sure it would be proper."

"Oh, for goodness' sake. I'm not going to make any inappropriate advances. I might be tempted but I promise I can control myself!"

"I need to look at my work diary. Chat to my boss, et cetera. I've also got to sort out my transport, don't forget."

"I'll drive you both ways. Not a problem. It would be great to show you Cornwall. I just know you'll love it.

"We'll see. You're very generous."

They spent a happy, rather lazy evening watching television. Carolyn put together a simple supper and they ate from trays, still watching.

Just after 10 o'clock, Jed rose and decided to leave for Paul's home.

"I'd better go now before I fall asleep. I'd hate to offend your moral principles by sleeping on your sofa."

She smiled, wondering if she should offer him a bed for the night, but decided against it.

"What time do you need me tomorrow morning?" he asked.

"If you're really sure, I need to be at work by nine-thirty. Can you be here at nine?"

"Not a problem. I'll see you then. Sleep well." He kissed her on the cheek and breezed out. "See you in the morning."

She leaned against the door when he had gone. Her mind was racing around the possibilities of leaving here the following week. What would everyone think?

It was a long way to go. Suppose they didn't get on? She'd be stuck there, without a car and any means of getting home again. And Jed might have to work. How would she feel about being left alone all day, with nowhere to go?

No, it was a foolish idea. She would tell him so the next morning. He was very kind and would undoubtedly put himself out considerably to accommodate her but she really felt it wouldn't be right. One day perhaps, one day in her uncertain future, she would go and stay somewhere and look him up. That would be quite enough, wouldn't it?

She went to bed and lay there for some time, wide awake with her brain racing round in circles. She even felt slightly guilty for enjoying life without Henry.

What was he doing? She hoped he was all right. Whatever he'd put her through, she still felt some affection for him.

It was a different feeling to forgiving him. That, she didn't think she would ever be able to do. But the memory of the fun they'd had, the good times they'd spent, it all meant something to her.

At last, she fell asleep and woke slightly late the next day.

Jed rang her doorbell promptly at nine o'clock. She let him in and said she'd be a minute or two.

"No worries," he said easily. "Did you sleep well?"

"Bit mixed," she told him. "I was too busy thinking."

"About Cornwall, I hope."

"Not really. I don't think it's such a good idea. Even if I can get time off work, I'd hate to be stuck somewhere without transport and... well, without my car."

"You could always use mine. I have a motorbike I sometimes use for work. Not that I have to work all the time. I've done a couple of big contracts lately so I can take time off. Two or three weeks easily. Oh, apart from next Sunday. I do have a commitment then, but you could always come with me."

It seemed every objection she'd thought of had been dismissed in a breath.

"I'll give it some more thought," she said. "Right, I'm ready. Let's go."

When they reached her office, he parked and asked when she'd like a lift anywhere.

"I don't know yet. In fact, I can't keep you sitting there all day. If I need to go anywhere, I'll borrow someone's car. I think

I shall be based here most of the day anyway. You go off and enjoy yourself."

"Well, if you're sure. What time do you finish?"

"About five. But don't worry about me. I can easily get a lift home. Someone will drop me off, I'm sure."

"I insist. I'll be here at five. Now, go and work hard so you can be free next week."

"You're impossible." She laughed. "But many thanks."

"Can I have your mobile number? In case I need it for anything?" She told him what it was and he punched it into his phone. "Great. Thanks. I'll send you a text so you'll have mine. Have a good day. Bye."

She said goodbye to him and went inside.

"Who's the new man?" one of her colleagues asked.

"A friend of my brother Paul's. My car was stolen and set on fire. It's a write-off."

"Oh, that's terrible! Whoever was responsible?"

"No idea. It was parked outside my brother's place on Saturday night and someone took it away. I'm going to have to get another one, I suppose."

"I'd continue to get lifts from the hunk, if I were you. He certainly looked an improvement on..." The girl stopped speaking at this point.

Carolyn knew exactly what she had been going to say and wanted to quell her embarrassment.

"It's OK. I can mention Henry's name without falling apart. He's in the past now."

"Brave of you. Now, I'd better get on. Have you got the Doreman file?"

The week had begun.

* * * *

At five o'clock precisely, Jed texted to say he was there and waiting for her. She texted him back to say she would be ten more minutes and that she could get a lift if he didn't want to wait. Naturally, he did want to wait.

As she came out of the office, he stepped out of his car.

"Hi, there. Good day?"

"Yes, thanks. You?"

"Not bad. I said we'd meet Paul later. I hope that's OK with you? Only he's on his own this week, Mel being away."

"Yes, of course. But if you guys want to do something on your own, don't worry about me. I'm used to being on my own."

He said nothing but simply smiled. They drove to her flat and he followed her inside.

"I assumed you'd want to change before we go bowling."

"Bowling?" she said in surprise.

"Indeed. We have a booking for seven-thirty then we're going to eat pizzas. Hope you approve."

"Well, yes. But like I said, you don't have to include me in everything."

"Of course we do. I want you to realise you're indispensable to my enjoyment of my week here. Did you organise your holiday for next week, by the way?"

"I'm still thinking about it," she told him, lying through her back teeth.

She had spoken to her boss who had immediately agreed to her going away. Carolyn wasn't all that convinced she should go. She might speak to Paul later, if she had the chance. He would know if she was being foolish or if she might enjoy it.

"Go and change. And hurry up. I want us to get there in good time and find some decent parking."

"Heavens, it's only just after six. I'll go and change. Put the kettle on, will you? I'm gasping for a cuppa."

He obediently put two tea bags into the mugs. He even remembered she drank it black.

Fire!

AS the week went on, Carolyn was more and more convinced she should go back to Cornwall with Jed. She had booked a week off, but didn't tell him that.

When she told him she was considering the trip after all, he was ridiculously pleased and swung her round in a circle, telling her she would not regret it.

"Well, I really hope not," she protested, laughing and suddenly feeling quite dizzy.

"I'll be on my best behaviour and promise I'll look after you. Will you be able to get time off work?"

"I've already booked it. I did it earlier in the week. I hadn't decided to come back with you at the time, mind you. I thought it might be a good idea to look at cars. The police told me it was definitely mine that had been burned out. The insurance company have agreed that I can get another one."

"Are you going for a new one? Or looking for an old one?"

"Unfortunately, I don't think they'll give me enough for a brand new one. Mine was only a couple of years old but new models cost so much more."

They discussed the opportunities available to her and decided to go and look at cars immediately. They drove to the nearby garage and wandered round their parking lot. Immediately, a salesman came out to help them, or rather hoping to make a sale.

"I expect you're ready to close soon, aren't you?" Carolyn asked.

"We can stay here for as long as you need. Don't worry. I'll leave you to look around and come back in a few minutes."

"Thank heavens for small mercies," she muttered when he'd left them. "Can't stand it when they hover round all the time."

"Me neither. I was about to tell him to get lost."

They looked at several of the cars and at last she decided she couldn't face it any longer.

"I'll say I'm thinking about it. Let's go and see him and then we can go home."

The salesman wanted them to sit down and talk about exactly what she wanted but she politely declined and together they left. Jed smiled at her.

"You're very good at not being pushed into anything, aren't you?"

"Maybe. Sometimes."

"Well, it's something I admire about you. I

was pretty pushy trying to get you to come to Cornwall and you waited till you were good and ready to agree," he remarked as they drove back to her flat.

"I booked the week off but thought I'd keep you waiting for a while. Don't want you getting complacent, now do I?"

"You're a bit of a tease, I'd say. But not to worry, you're coming and that's all I could have hoped for. I must phone my cleaning lady. Make sure it's all spotless and ready for my esteemed guest."

"Don't go to any trouble on my account," Carolyn insisted.

"Oh, I won't. I need to let her know when I'm coming back anyway. I thought we could set off early on Saturday if that's OK with you?"

"How early?"

"I'd like to make it as soon after seven as you can be up."

"Seven? Wow! I'd better pack tomorrow evening. No going out tomorrow, then. You can spend the evening with Paul on your own. He is your friend, after all."

"OK. I suppose we'll manage without you. What do you fancy doing this evening?"

"I ought to put some washing on. Then I can iron tomorrow evening."

"All right. I'll give you five minutes to do that then we'll go and collect Paul. Maybe go to a nice pub for our last meal all together."

She actually took almost fifteen minutes. Jed was stomping round after her, grumbling at being kept waiting.

"Don't be so impatient. I need to have everything clean before I go."

"I do have a washing machine and I understand one can easily buy soap powder in Cornwall. For goodness' sake, woman, come on."

"Just a minute more. I need to get something from my room."

"It's almost seven o'clock. Paul will think we're lost." He was speaking to an empty space as she was bustling around in the bedroom.

"Right. Ready."

"I hope it won't take you this long on Saturday. I want to get on the road. We'll stop for breakfast at a place I know. Wonderful bacon baps."

"With or without butter?"

"With butter, of course. Why do you ask?"

"Just winding you up." She laughed.

It was a jolly evening. There was a folk singer playing and they all joined in with the choruses. Paul had a lovely voice and thoroughly enjoyed himself.

Jed's voice was surprisingly good. He also

sang with some gusto. They ate chilli and rice and drank beers. At the end of it all, they drove back to her flat.

"That was such a good evening. Thank you both for including me," Carolyn said. "I won't invite you in as I must sort out my laundry. 'Night, both of you."

"'Night, Carolyn. I'll be round for nine in the morning. Your lift to work?" Jed told her. She'd looked at him blankly.

"Oh, yes, of course. Thanks a lot."

"No worries."

"'Night, Paul. When's Mel back by the way?"

"Saturday at some ungodly hour in the morning."

"Hope Jed doesn't get in her way. You know he's picking me up at seven?"

"Oh, dear, no, I didn't. It'll be a short night then, won't it?"

"Nah. I'll see myself off," Jed reassured him. "We're going to stop for breakfast on the way so we won't need to do anything first. Anyway, we'd better let this lady do her stuff. 'Bye for now."

****

By the next morning, most of Carolyn's stuff was dry and she piled it into her laundry basket. She would have a busy evening getting everything ready for her trip. She grabbed some toast and drank her tea and was ready for Jed when he arrived. She ran down the stairs and met him in the car park.

"You're on time today," he remarked.

"Practising for tomorrow. Actually, I've got a rather busy day ahead. I need to get everything sorted so my colleagues can answer any client questions that may come up."

"All sounds very efficient. Right. Let's go."

When they arrived at her workplace, they met a lot of people standing outside.

Carolyn got out of the car and went over to the group.

"What's going on?"

"There's a fire. The fire brigade are on their way. We're all only just arriving and found some of the computers are burning. The smell is terrible and the whole place is likely to catch fire."

"Oh, heavens, not another fire. I expect we all have to stay out till... oh, here they come."

The fire brigade arrived amid the sound of sirens and with blue lights flashing.

"Who's in charge here?" one of them asked.

"I suppose I am," Carolyn's boss Emily said.

Emily was an older lady who never really wanted to be in charge and usually let her staff make most of the decisions.

"Can you tell me what's happening in there?" As the fireman was speaking, the rest of the crew were unfurling yards of hose and getting ready to go inside.

"It seems as if the computers are all burning…"

"Hold on, chaps. Electrical fire." At this point there was a huge roar and the whole office seemed to be ablaze. "OK, looks like we do need water. Keep back, everyone."

The windows shattered as the flames reached them. The fire crew started to spray water in through the doors and windows and slowly, the flames died back. They pushed inside and gradually, the fire was doused. The chief came back to speak to the anxious group.

"I'm afraid the damage looks pretty devastating. There's nothing left. What was your business?"

"Home interior design. Have we really lost everything?" someone asked.

"I'm afraid so. I don't know if there was a fireproof safe?"

"Well, yes, there was one in my office. It couldn't possibly have survived though. Not in all that flame." The boss was very sceptical.

"One of us will take a look later, once it's cooled down a bit and we can get inside. You say it seemed to be the computers that were burning?"

"Yes," one of the others said. "They were smoking and suddenly burst into flames. We were only just getting here at the time."

"Do you leave them on all the time?"

"Yes. On standby."

"OK. I'll let the investigators know. They'll be round later. I think you might as well all go home. There's nothing you can do here," the fireman pointed out.

"Let's go to the coffee bar. Discuss our options," Emily said. "Dreadful business. What a loss." She really did look terribly shocked and rather pale.

"Are you all right?" Carolyn asked. "You don't look very well."

"It's just shock, I'm afraid."

"Well, take care, won't you?"

"I will. Let's leave these gentlemen to do their work."

Jed stepped forward.

"Do you want me to hang around for a bit? I don't have anything planned."

"If you like. I don't expect we'll be there for long. Then I suppose we shall all go home. There isn't much to be done here. It seems terrible."

"At least you won't be missing anything

when we're in Cornwall."

"Oh, I couldn't possibly leave at this time. I'm sorry, Jed, but we shall need to reorganise everything. There are clients we need to contact and we'll need somewhere to work."

Jed looked totally nonplussed.

"Surely..."

"I'm sorry. But you must understand."

"Excuse me," Emily interrupted. "You must go, Carolyn. There won't be anything left for anyone to do. If the discs are in the safe and usable, I can send out a blanket e-mail from my laptop to the clients to say everything's on hold. We shall undoubtedly lose a few of them who want things done yesterday but that's their problem. To be honest, I'm not sure I shall even continue the business. I need time to think it through."

"I see," Carolyn replied. "But you'll surely need some help?"

"Not at all. I'm not sure how long I can go on paying all of you. I think it's best if you all have notice from now on. I'll let you know what I can pay you when the insurance claim goes through. Forget the coffee bar. Go home, all of you."

She turned away from the group and was clearly very upset. She looked dreadful and Carolyn was concerned about her.

"Emily, please sit down in your car. You look awful. I don't want you fainting or something. Jed, can you help me to get her to her car?"

"She can't possibly drive in her state," he told her.

"I could drive her home in her car," Carolyn offered.

"And I can follow you to bring you home."

The rest of the group were all talking earnestly, debating what they were going to do. They were all concerned about their boss who was very popular, if not terribly dynamic.

It was clear they all looked up to Carolyn as the natural successor.

"I'll take Emily home now," she addressed the group. "I'd suggest you all go home, too, and wait to see what tomorrow brings. Or Monday, should I say."

The group left the building to its smoky demise and slowly and quietly got into their cars and drove away. Carolyn was not happy about deserting the company at this point but it didn't make sense to be hanging around doing very little.

She drove competently to Emily's home, quite a long way from the office. Jed was following her and stopped a little way behind her. She helped Emily out of the car and asked for her keys.

"Oh, dear me," Emily kept saying. "Why?"

"It seems to have been a complete accident. Have you got the insurance details at home? You can phone them."

"I have but I don't feel they're going to take it seriously."

"Whyever not? It was an accident. Horrible but an accident."

"Was it, though? I'm not so sure."

"What on earth do you mean?"

"Forget what I said. Of course it was an accident. I'm talking through my hat. Now, I'm feeling better so you can go off with that boyfriend of yours. Enjoy your trip to Cornwall."

"You're absolutely sure I shouldn't stay and help you to sort things out?"

"Of course I'm sure. Go on. Enjoy it."

"OK, I will. But promise me you'll take it easy. Don't come to any decisions in a hurry. Do you want me to see you inside?"

"No, thanks. I'm fine now. It was really just the shock. And forget what I said about accidents or not. Of course it was an accident."

Carolyn walked back to Jed's car deep in thought. She was troubled by Emily's words, which to her sounded as though she knew something. That something was not quite as it seemed.

She mentioned it to Jed as they drove to her flat.

"It almost seemed as if she was expecting something to happen. She was asking herself if it really was an accident. What do you think she meant?"

"No idea. Perhaps she felt she shouldn't have left the computers turned on. They should have been fine, but you never know."

"Maybe. We've never had a problem before. They've always been left on. Oh dear, I really don't like leaving at this point in time."

"Stop it," Jed said firmly. "We're going to go to Cornwall in the morning. Tonight if you prefer. You could always go and pack right now and we can set off this afternoon. How about it?"

"I couldn't possibly. I have a stack of ironing to do and then I need to decide what I'm taking."

"Bring it with you. I've got a perfectly good iron. Paul was busy tonight anyway so I was only going to be sitting by myself."

"But I've got sheets and other stuff to do."

"Do them when you get back. You won't have to go to work. Come on. Let's go and get you packed. I'll leave a note for Paul and we can easily be in Cornwall by the evening."

"You make it sound tempting."

"Then be tempted. There's nothing to keep us here."

She glanced at her watch. It was only just after ten o'clock. Could she possibly do everything and be ready to go?

"OK. Drop me at home. Then go and pack and come back and pick me up. Cornwall, here we come."

"That's wonderful. I promise you won't be disappointed. I'll do as you ask and be back to collect you at eleven-thirty."

"That's much too soon," Carolyn protested.

"Be ready or I'll go on my own and leave you behind."

He stopped outside her flat and left her to go and pack.

"You'll only need shorts and T-shirts – oh, and some swimming stuff for the beach. And best to pack some warm clothes for the evening. It can get chilly. Bring something for wet weather, too. It does rain just occasionally in Cornwall. I'll see you at eleven-thirty."

She ran up the stairs and let herself in. She felt slightly panicked and started dashing round. She stopped herself and took out the ironing board. Half an hour later, she had ironed most of the things she planned to pack and put them into her suitcase.

She stuffed the board away and left the rest of her ironing for when she got back. She could hardly think that far ahead.

Fridge. She needed to check what was in there and turn it off. For the next quarter of an hour she worked very hard, putting perishables into a carrier bag. She was almost ready when Jed rang her doorbell.

"Nearly done. Just need to check the windows are all shut."

"I'll do that."

"Thanks. I think that's about it. I'm done. Anything that's left will be here when I get back. Have you told Paul your latest mad scheme?"

"I called him at work. He didn't mind and seemed fine. I've even left his keys in the kitchen."

"Very good. My case is ready to put in the car. And there a carrier bag with odd bits and pieces in. We can use them up, can't we?"

"Definitely. Anything to feed us over the next few days."

"Hardly that. Just some fruit and a few bits of vegetables. I've been running it down this week ready to leave tomorrow."

He went downstairs carrying her bag and she looked round. She loved her flat. It had been carefully decorated to fit in with her lifestyle. Uncluttered and simple and a prime example of her work.

For a moment she thought about Henry and wondered where he was hiding. It had all been so strange the way he had disappeared so suddenly. Why hadn't he even tried to contact her?

She gave a sigh. Henry was part of her past now. She may never know what had happened to him.

She minded not knowing where he was and what was happening in his life. Perhaps he had found someone else and cancelled the wedding for that reason. But she would never actually believe that. They had been much too close for her to fail to know something like that.

"Oh, Henry," she muttered. "I really hope you're all right."

She went out and locked the door and ran down to Jed and a week in Cornwall.

Perfect Timing...

IT took three and a half hours to reach Exeter. Carolyn had fallen asleep when Jed stopped the car. She jolted awake.

"Where are we?" she asked.

"Exeter services. I needed a break. Had a good sleep?"

"I suppose I must have done. How much further is it?"

"A couple of hours or thereabouts. Maybe a bit less. Depends on the traffic. You want something to eat?"

"I am pretty peckish. Motorway services, though. Ugh!"

"Don't be a snob. Come on, get out. We'll see what they've got. There are various stores on the site. We can do some shopping for supper. I thought you'd prefer to eat at home after the journey."

"Sounds perfect."

It was very busy and took them a while to get served. They had a sandwich and coffee and they sat outside to eat them. Then they went into the store and bought steak and some salad and a loaf of bread. Jed insisted on paying as she was his guest.

"Keep your money. You might need it if

you haven't got a job any more."

She frowned.

"You're right. I somehow doubt Emily is going to start up again. I suspect she's been ready to retire for quite a while now. I suppose I'll have to start looking again. I shouldn't find it too hard. I'm still youngish and well experienced. It's a case of finding a company with a vacancy."

"You could always start on your own."

"Oh, yes, of course. Like heck I could!" She smiled a rather wry smile. "I'll wait and see what happens. Gosh, when I think of that burned-out wreck of a place and compare it to what was once there. Horrific."

"You should try to stop thinking about it."

They drove on to the A30.

"This is where I feel I'm getting closer. It seems sort of peaceful, don't you think?"

"I suppose so, yes. The mad traffic has calmed down at least."

"Quite a long way to go yet. You can go back to sleep if you want to," Jed suggested.

"I don't even know where you live."

"In a tiny village in the far west. Only about half a dozen houses. I'm currently renting my place from a local farmer. I'd really like to buy it but he's not willing to sell. It's quite an old cottage actually. Not unlike Paul and Mel's place."

"Sounds nice."

"I love it there. This time of year is rather lovely in Cornwall. Lots of wildflowers around. The bird life is good, too. Lots of baby birds learning to fly."

"Perfect for a photographer."

It was almost seven o'clock by the time they arrived at Tregorwen. They decided to unpack the car and Jed would start cooking.

"I'll show you your room and you can unpack if you like," Jed offered.

"Wouldn't you like some help with dinner?"

"From what you say about your cooking skills, I can probably manage better on my own. But thanks for the offer." He grinned.

"I'm pretty good at salad. And I can lay tables quite satisfactorily."

He took her upstairs and showed her into a small but perfect bedroom. It was pretty but not fussy and she loved the plain blue curtains against a matching striped wallpaper. There was a double bed taking up most of the space and a small wardrobe and drawers to one side.

He dumped her case on the bed.

"After you've unpacked, I'll have a glass of something ready for you when you come down," he promised. "Oh, the bathroom is over there. You can look at my room, too, if you're interested."

He had guessed exactly what she planned to do. She grinned and said she'd be down in a few minutes.

Carolyn peered through the tiny window. She could see a strip of bright blue sea in the distance. Immediately outside her window was a pretty garden with a delightful mixture of flowers spilling out of borders on to the small lawn.

She must ask him how much was already here when he moved in and how much he had done. Was it all his furniture or the cottage owners?

She opened her case and hung her clothes in the wardrobe on the plentiful supply of hangers. Suddenly, the waft of onions cooking floated up the stairs and her tummy rumbled. She stuffed the rest of her things into the drawers and rushed downstairs.

"Glass of red OK for you?" Jed asked.

"Wonderful, thank you. Can I do something to help?"

"Sit and talk to me."

"Oh, I can do that all right. Talking for Britain is what I do best."

"What do you think of the cottage?" he asked.

"It's really lovely. The farmer obviously has

good taste."

"What do you mean?"

"I assume he or his wife was responsible for the furniture and decoration?"

"Nope. That was all me. It was pretty much of a wreck when I found it. This represents many hours of hard labour. I get it for a pittance in rent to make up for it. The problem is, he expects it's now worth a lot of money but, hopefully, he won't sell it until I'm ready to leave. The other problem is, I think I like it here and don't see myself ready to move any time soon."

"Perhaps you should get a valuation from an estate agent or three. See what they think it may be worth and then you can make him an offer."

"I doubt I could afford any sort of offer he'd accept. When it was a wreck, it was quite different. I could have afforded it in those days."

"How long did it take you?"

"About eighteen months altogether. I was camping here for a lot of the time. He paid for most of the basic stuff and I bought the furniture and did the decorating. Glad you like it, anyway. Right, we're just about ready to eat. There's cutlery in the drawer beside you."

Carolyn took out knives and forks and put them on the table. He produced a bowl of salad from the fridge. Goodness knew when he'd made that, she thought.

As she dug her knife into the steak, she gave him a huge grin.

"This looks delicious," she said. "Thank you so much."

"My pleasure entirely. Tomorrow, I'll show you round the area. There are some lovely little coves near here. Almost secret sort of places that few people know about."

"Lovely."

It was a pleasant evening and by 10 o'clock they were both yawning and decided to have an early night.

She fell asleep quickly, dreaming about what had seemed an endless journey in the car.

****

Unknown to either of them, Henry was living about five miles away. In another small hamlet he'd rented a tiny cottage and had even found himself a job, working in a small shop. It was far different from anything he'd ever done before and he was rather enjoying the lack of responsibility and being able to get up each morning without any worries.

Without worries was perhaps a slight exaggeration. He was constantly looking over his shoulder, expecting to see someone from his old life chasing him. He felt reasonably safe in his hidden corner of the county and felt content.

Henry still felt guilty about the horrendous way he had treated the woman he'd believed he loved, but he hadn't managed to pluck up the courage to contact her.

He wasn't bothered by the fact he'd left some of his possessions in their flat. It had always been Carolyn's flat anyway. It was her inheritance that had bought it and though he had helped with painting and simple stuff, it had always been her choice that won out in the end. Whatever he'd done to hurt her, Henry hoped she'd forgiven him and wasn't sitting at home alone brooding over him.

He put on his shirt with the slogan of the shop written on the pocket and set off for his day's work. The shop's owner had also let him the cottage so it was a convenient arrangement all round.

She was waiting for him to arrive and said she was going out for the day.

"My grandchildren need looking after so I hope you don't mind looking after things for me. There's a delivery coming at some point but I doubt you'll be so busy you can't see to it. OK?"

"That's fine. Shall I unpack it?"

"If you've got the time. Check it all, then you can put it in the stock room."

"Right you are, Demelza. Have a nice day and don't worry about the shop. I can easily manage it."

He did actually think life would be easier if she wasn't there, fussing round. He got on with her quite well but she was always chatting and asking him things about his past.

He'd invented quite a past for himself. He'd been widowed about two years ago and was trying to rediscover himself. This was proving a perfect opportunity.

At times, Henry was almost believing his story himself. It was a rather solitary life but he had a television and an iPod and felt he needed this time and space.

Someone came into the shop and he had started his day.

* * * *

Back at Jed's home, they were waking to a lovely morning. Carolyn got up first, went downstairs and took a mug of coffee out into the garden. There were birds singing and she could hear the buzz of bees as they searched for nectar among the roses. The sun felt warm on her shoulders and she wondered if she ought to go and find her sunglasses. She stretched lazily out and felt very content.

In some ways, she felt she was over Henry and that was undoubtedly due to this new man, Jed. But how did she really feel about him? He was lovely, she thought. In time, she might even find him most attractive but it was too soon. Too soon after Henry.

What was he doing, she wondered. His expertise in computers would surely mean he'd easily get another job. She had no idea where on earth he was. He may even have gone abroad somewhere – Hong Kong or Singapore.

She'd got over hating him for what he had done. In fact, he might even have done her a favour. It would have terrible if they had got married and then wanted to split up.

"I hope you're all right, Henry," she whispered.

"Talking to yourself?" Jed asked, as he came into the garden. "I saw you'd boiled the kettle so I've made some coffee for me, too. Lovely morning, isn't it?"

"Certainly is."

"Did you sleep well?"

"Marvellous, thank you. How about you?"

"Yes, fine. What do you want to eat? I can offer you toast, toast or even toast."

"Toast might be a good choice, thanks."

"Good girl. Toast it is. I'll go and sort it."

"I'll come and help."

"No. You stay there. You make a nice picture against the garden flowers. I might even dig out my camera."

"Don't you dare! I'm in no state to be photographed."

"I don't agree. I like pictures of people being relaxed. I must show you some of my more relaxed pictures sometime. You stay there. I won't be long."

She sat where she was, feeling distinctly lazy. In a few minutes, Jed came out with a tray, which he set down on the small table.

"Come and get it. I've made some more coffee. Proper stuff this time and none of your instant. Toast and honey do for you?"

"Lovely. But you really don't need to wait on me, you know."

"I'm happy to do it. But after today, you can take a share while I do some work. I need to take a few pictures for a company who want brochures and a website to promote their holiday letting business. You can come along if you're interested or I can drop you somewhere to wander."

"Sounds good. I'll tag along with you. Tomorrow, you say?" She was spreading delicious gold honey on her toast and then took a mouthful.

"Oh, wow! I've died and gone to heaven. What sort of honey is this?"

"It's a local heather honey. I buy it at a little shop I know."

"It's wonderful. I must take some back with me."

"We'll call in sometime during the week."

They chatted for some time, planning their day.

"Actually, I might need to do some shopping quite soon," Jed said. "Apart from the basics, there's very little to eat in the place. I have got a small freezer but it's practically empty from before I went away."

"Looks like it's the supermarket first, then. Then perhaps we can walk down to the sea?" Carolyn suggested. "Doesn't look too far from here."

"OK. We'll do just that." Jed nodded.

"And please, let me buy some of the stuff. If I'm going to be eating it, that seems fair to me."

"You don't have a job any more. You need to save the pennies. You don't know when you'll be working again."

Carolyn frowned. She'd forgotten about the fire and the implications and felt almost sick when she remembered it.

"I wonder how Emily is? Hope she's not feeling too down in the dumps. Maybe I should call her."

"I'd leave her to get over it for the weekend."

"Oh, goodness. I'd quite forgotten it was Saturday. Do you really have to work tomorrow? It'll be Sunday."

"Afraid so. Tomorrow is changeover day and the only time the properties will be vacant for an hour or two. I need to get inside and take some shots. If I go around lunchtime, they'll be cleaned and ready for the next lot to come in."

"Quite complicated, isn't it?"

"They're quite good clients. They own a lot of properties around this part of the county. Often renew their brochures so more pictures for me. Right. If you've had enough to eat and drink, shall we go?"

"Shall I wash up?"

"Nah. We'll do it all together later. Come on. Let's go and hit the local town. There's even a choice of supermarkets."

They drove to Penzance and decided to have a walk in the town before shopping. The harbour looked delightful in the sunshine. He led her up to the top of the stairs in the shopping precinct and looked over the wall.

"Oh, my! That's such a good view. So many little boats in there. Oh, it's so lovely." She sniffed the sea air, loving it.

"You want to look in the shops in the town?"

"A little look, perhaps. But I do want to

go to the sea."

They walked through the arcade and into Market Jew Street. There were a number of empty shops.

"It looks as if it's got the same disease as home," Carolyn remarked. "So many shops closing down, presumably because of the business rates."

"Well, that and lack of decent business. Not much fun being a shopkeeper these days, is it?"

"I suppose not. Maybe I won't open a shop, after all," she said with a laugh.

"I'd wondered whether to open somewhere myself. Sell some of my pictures and maybe make some cards, too. If I did, I'd need someone to manage the shop while I was out taking pictures. You don't fancy doing that, do you?" he said jokingly.

"Pay me enough and I might. Come on, let's leave this lot and go and paddle. Well, maybe we should go shopping first if we want to eat again."

It was an interesting experience for Carolyn. Seeing how different people did their shopping fascinated her. She often pottered round quite slowly, looking at the different things and making her decision.

With Jed, there was no hesitation. He walked along each aisle and picked up what he wanted with no thought for looking at different choices.

"You like ice-cream?" he asked.

"Love it."

"Good. What sort?"

"I don't mind."

"Right. I'll get this one, then. It'll do as a sweet. I'm not really into sweets."

"Nor me. But ice-cream sounds wonderful."

"Good. Anything else you'd like?"

"I think you've got everything."

"I just need some fruit. Can't have you fainting away for lack of vitamins. Right. Let's get this show on the road."

They soon were home again and unpacked the shopping. Once everything was put away, Jed looked at the time.

"Heavens. It's almost half-past two. You must be starving."

"I am pretty hungry," she admitted.

"We'll go down to the beach and pick up some pasties. Nothing like sitting on a Cornish beach eating pasties."

They set off to walk down to the beach. There was a little shop just on the road down and they bought pasties.

"Gosh, they smell wonderful. Can't we eat them as we walk along?"

"Be my guest." They munched them, holding them in the paper bags.

"My first genuine Cornish pasty. They do

really taste different here," she said as she screwed up the bag. "Must be the Cornish air."

"Guess so. And we're not even on the beach yet."

It was a beautiful cove – very small and quiet and only one other family on the beach. Carolyn was speechless until he asked what she thought of it.

"It's so lovely. I can really see why you are so in love with the place."

"Loving is easy with somewhere like this," he said enigmatically.

He knew he was beginning to fall in love with this woman but he didn't want to say anything... not just yet. He knew she was still vulnerable and didn't want to frighten her off.

But he really hoped they might have a future together. The timing was perfect. She hadn't got a job and she was here, in his place, in his own surroundings.

Caution, Jed, he told himself severely. Don't let yourself say or do anything that will ruin things.

Early Days

JED was up early the next morning, sorting out his cameras ready for his job later. Carolyn heard him put the kettle on and stretched lazily. She really ought to get up but she felt warm and cosy here in her bed. The sun was shining behind her curtains, giving a blue haze to her room. She heard Jed coming upstairs and he tapped at her door.

"Come in," she called. "I'm still in bed."

"I've brought you some breakfast," he said, manoeuvring his way through her door with a tray.

"Goodness," she said, sitting up in surprise. "I thought it was just a cup of coffee or tea."

"I need to get moving before too long. It'll take me a while to drive over to the village and I don't want to be late. You don't have to come if you'd prefer to stay here."

"No, I want to come. I was just being lazy."

"Right. Well, enjoy breakfast and I'll see you later."

"Thanks very much," she said.

She buttered the toast and enjoyed more

of the delicious local honey, washed down with excellent coffee. She felt rather luxurious, lying there. It was most unusual for her to feel spoilt like this. She certainly couldn't remember Henry ever doing anything like this for her.

She thought about Jed. He was certainly a catch for someone. He was good-looking, easy company and certainly very kind.

Then she thought about his fiancée, or rather ex-fiancée. Carolyn realised she was actually quite glad she had gone off and left him. Even if it was too soon for Carolyn to consider him as anything more than a friend...

If they did get together at any time, it couldn't be for a while or people would say it was on the rebound, and there was no way anyone was going to say that about her.

She finished her toast and moved the tray to one side. It was time to get moving.

****

They drove along the main road until he turned off into what looked little more than a narrow cart track. There was even grass growing along its middle.

"I hope you know where we're going," she commented.

"I think it's down here. I haven't been here before but this sounds like the place she described when she phoned me. We should see some buildings quite soon." They drove on some way and then suddenly found themselves in a wide courtyard with several buildings round the edge.

"This looks a bit of all right, don't you think?"

"It looks gorgeous. A real haven."

"Well, that's exactly what it's called – Haven Holiday Homes."

"Very appropriate. Looks as if the cleaners are still working in some of the places."

"I expect they'll be here for quite a while. I'll work round them. Now, are you ready to be my assistant?"

"Don't ask me to photograph anything," she squeaked in alarm. "Put me behind a camera and I cut off everyone's heads."

"I was thinking you could help me to carry stuff in. Look after the tripods and so on."

"I think I might manage that. I'll even try not to drop anything."

"Good start. OK, I'll go and see the boss first and see where she wants us to start. Come on. I'll introduce you as my chief assistant."

She rather liked feeling a part if it all and followed him across the courtyard. He knocked at the door of the largest house and was soon answered.

"Yes? Oh, Mr Soames."

"Jed, please. This is my assistant, Carolyn. Meet Mrs James."

"How do you do," Carolyn said. "What a lovely place you have here," she added.

"Thank you. We've done it all ourselves. It was once a series of old barns and I saw the potential in converting them. We found some good builders locally and here we are. But do come inside."

They followed her in through a delightful hall with stone flags on the floor and several brightly coloured rugs.

"Come into the lounge. Or if you don't mind, come into the kitchen and I'll make some coffee while we discuss the photographs."

"Thanks very much. I just need to know exactly what sort of images you need and how they're going to be used."

The kitchen was every woman's dream. Oak fittings all round the large area, with every convenience one could think of. Mrs James went over to one of the sinks and pushed cups under a tap.

"Hope you don't mind instant. This tap is so much quicker than the machine," she remarked, filling the mugs with boiling water.

"That's terrific. Boiling water on tap."

Carolyn was impressed.

"Saves a lot of time. Now, sugar and milk are there. Help yourselves."

Carolyn sat quietly listening to them discussing the new website Jed was to create and the brochure Mrs James wanted. She was impressed by Jed's professionalism but then, it was his business.

"So, if you would like to send me your text, I'll incorporate it and send you the proofs back. Once approved, we can go live."

"So how long might this take?"

"I could start work on it right away and the website could be live in, well, as short a time as you like. Couple of days?"

"That's amazing. It'll probably take me a day or two to put words together."

They went on to discuss the various units on the site and what was required in the way of pictures. There were four separate buildings and each one was quite different. Carolyn was beginning to get quite excited by the thought of looking at them.

Mrs James picked up several bunches of keys and showed them round the various buildings. The cleaners were all working so it was a case of looking round first and deciding where to take pictures.

"Right, I think I have the gist of what you need. We'll need several pictures of the interiors, to show the rooms," Jed said. "I'll take some pictures of the whole courtyard and perhaps we can incorporate a click device to pick out individual properties. Then you can click on it to enter each one separately."

He considered.

"Yes, I'll try that and send it to you for your approval. What I need from you is a general introduction and a sheet of costs. I can put this in as appropriate. Now, I'll get my cameras."

"Golly, I'm so glad I picked you. You are exactly what I needed. Go for it. I can't wait." Mrs James obviously liked everything he'd said and was ready to go with whatever he suggested.

"My husband will be delighted he doesn't have to deal with it." She smiled. "Take whatever pictures you need. I'd like some of each property – bedrooms, living-room and kitchen. I leave it to you."

"Fine. I'll sort it all out and let you see what I've taken afterwards."

They went to the car and he picked up several bags with cameras and lights and asked Carolyn to carry some of them. He set about making his pictures count and took several of each setting.

She was amazed at the amount of time it took and watched, fascinated. It was almost three o'clock before he pronounced himself satisfied.

"Good. That'll do me nicely," he told her. "Come on. Let's say goodbye and get on our way. Sorry it took so long. You must be starving."

"I am peckish."

They went to the main house to say goodbye.

"Come in. I've put a few snacks together for you. You must be feeling hungry by now," Mrs James said. "Nothing special, of course."

"That's very good of you," Carolyn said as they followed her into the kitchen. "Nothing special? It looks like a proper feast to me."

There was pâté, ham and salad and a delicious looking crusty loaf of bread.

"This is terrific. Thank you very much," Jed echoed her feelings.

Soon they were both sitting with full plates and enjoying the unexpected treat. Mrs James ate with them, commenting that she hadn't expected them to take quite so long.

"I had to make sure the lighting was right and get proper angles. It makes all the difference to the results if you get it all right. I hope you'll like what I've done."

"I'm sure it will be perfect. Are you sure

the price you quoted will cover your work?"

"Of course. Besides, you're feeding us rather well, too."

"But your web design, that will take you extra time, surely. I'd be happy to pay you for it."

"I'll see how long it takes. But don't worry about it. I won't charge much more anyway."

When they had all eaten as much as they wanted, they thanked her and left the lovely property.

"Who would know all that is hidden down that little lane?" Carolyn remarked. "You ought to have taken a picture of the entrance to the lane, otherwise people will find it tricky to find."

"Gosh, yes, why didn't I think of that? Do you mind if we go back? Won't take long. Just a quick stop and a quick snap."

He turned the car round and went back to the entrance to the property. He parked a little way along the road, picked up a camera and ran back. He seemed to have taken several shots, she thought.

When they were home again, he seemed rather distracted as he asked her what she wanted to do.

"I suspect you want to download your films and see what you've taken. Am I right?" She smiled.

He looked rather shamefaced.

"I am keen to make sure the pictures are all good."

"Then do it. I'm fine. I might go for a walk. Or just sit out in the garden."

"If you're sure. I'll organise something for supper later on."

"Don't worry about it. Go on, off you go and sort out your pictures."

Without further ado, he put on his computer and started to download his morning's work. She listened to his disgruntled mutterings and then his appreciative sounds.

She shook her head and went outside.

It was a lovely early evening and she sat quietly listening to the birds and enjoying the peace. She dozed off and awoke some time later feeling somewhat chilly.

She went inside and saw that Jed was working with deep concentration. She looked over his shoulder and was very impressed.

"Oh, hi. What time is it?" he asked.

"Nearly seven."

"Oh, dear. I'd better stop doing this and find something for supper."

"If you don't mind me rummaging in your freezer, I'll make something."

"Don't mind at all. But are you sure you can manage? I'd rather come and do it myself than clear up some burned remains."

"Cheek! I can do simple things. I'll see what I can find."

"There may be some fish in the there. You can't go far wrong with that." He turned back to his computer screen.

An hour later, she came back into the room, saying supper was ready when he was. He came into the kitchen and proudly, she drew her fish pie out of the oven.

"Wow," he commented, "that looks wonderful!"

"See? I can cook some things. OK, I admit I cheated a bit. Used a can of soup instead of making sauce, but I hope you like it."

"I'm sure I'll love it. Makes a change having someone else to cook for me. I appreciate it."

When they had cleared the dishes, he invited her to come and look at the work he'd been doing. She sat at his computer, clicked through his pictures.

"These really are very good. You've made everywhere look so appealing."

"Click on one of the doors and see what happens," he invited.

She did and was immediately taken into each of the properties in turn.

"That's terrific. You're very clever. At least as good as Henry... Sorry, I should never have said that."

"It's OK. I'll take it as a compliment. I'm sure you meant it as such."

"It was his job," Carolyn said. "He made his living by working on computers so of course he was good. But it's not fair of me to compare the two of you."

"I used to. Make my living on computers, I mean. I know how to manipulate things to get the results I want."

"I didn't realise. What made you give that up?"

"My ex worked in the same company. I sort of went off in a flurry of bad temper and decided to change everything. I followed my dream and took up photography in earnest. I also felt this was the perfect location for my new profession. I'm happy now and don't have anyone else to worry about. At least..."

"At least what?"

"Oh, nothing. So, you like what I've done so far? The pictures, I mean."

"I think they're terrific. I'm sure Mrs J will be delighted."

"Thanks. I hope so. I don't think there's much more I can do now, so let's relax. Anything on television?"

"The usual Sunday night stuff."

"Let's slump, then. I do feel weary after all our efforts today. Let's sit and watch something and decide what we're doing tomorrow."

"Suits me fine. I do feel a bit sleepy. Must be the Cornish air. Haven't done anything really."

"Lots of folk say the air is tiring. Maybe it's just that you've stopped working so hard."

"Gosh, yes. I wonder what sort of weekend Emily has had. Not good, I bet."

"Maybe not but, unfortunately, there isn't a great deal you can do. Try to relax and stop worrying."

****

The next few days went by in a whirl. They visited lots of local places and some more distant ones. Wherever he went, Jed carried his camera. He took lots of pictures which Carolyn thought were excellent but he wasn't satisfied with many of them and deleted them. She felt amazed he could do that so frequently, but he complained something wasn't quite right or he'd got the wrong angle.

"I'd be delighted to have done anything half so good," she told him.

"I'll show you some of the ones I'm really pleased with. Then you'll see the difference."

She realised she was really beginning to

feel something for this admittedly rather gorgeous man. He'd never tried to even to kiss her, for which she felt truly grateful. She still felt it was early days since her breakup from Henry.

He obviously respected her feelings.

That evening, Jed took a large file from the bookshelf.

"Here are some of my favourite pictures. Look at them and you'll see why I deleted so many of the ones I took recently. These are so much better." He passed a series of large photos to her one by one.

"Oh, my goodness! These are wonderful." She looked through them all and was lost for words. "You really are very good. I thought your pictures of the buildings we visited were excellent but these are quite outstanding. You could win prizes with some of them."

He seemed to blush and looked away.

"You have won prizes, haven't you?" she asked.

"I did, yes."

"What did you win?"

"Well... I did win quite a substantial cheque in a major competition. But it's living in such a beautiful place that is beneficial. It's the scenery, not me."

"Which picture won?"

"I've only got a small copy. It was a sunset.

Hang on, I'll find it in a minute."

He foraged through another folder and produced a most glorious picture of a sunset. It was a deep magenta, tinged with oranges and a cerulean blue tipping the picture at the bottom.

"Goodness. How did you manage to capture that one? The sea looks amazing over the bottom of it. Where was it?"

"Just outside here. It was taken in early spring and was at the end of a perfect day. If there had been any clouds they would have been a pinky orange colour. But there weren't on this occasion. Hence I could capture the whole scene in its perfection. I have to admit, I was very pleased – raised my profile somewhat."

"I should think so. I have to say, I'm impressed. You have a real talent for composition. How on earth do you get everything into the picture?"

"It's the way I look at things," he said with a smile. "Anyway, there are loads more if you really want to see them."

"Yes, please. I've always loved seeing people's holiday pictures but these are in quite a different category. These are studies people would want to hang on their walls."

"I've had some canvas prints made and they're hanging in various places around. I make a bit out of each one. That keeps me going, together with special commissions, like the brochure and website I'm doing for Mrs James. Reminds me, I still haven't had her approval for the stuff I sent her. Excuse me a minute. I'll e-mail her and check that she's received it all."

Carolyn sat looking through more of his pictures. She loved the ones of trees and grasses. Close-ups of some leaves and flowers were equally inspiring.

At last, Jed came back to sit beside her, saying Mrs James had loved all he'd done and was more than ready for him to take the stuff for the brochure to the printers.

"We'll go tomorrow if that's OK. I'll show you some of the delights of Truro. It's a nice town actually. Quite busy and with lots of small shops independently owned. There are the large retail chains there, too, of course, but it's the smaller places that give it character."

"I'll look forward to it. Now, I don't know about you, but I wouldn't mind an early night."

"If that's what you want to do. I might stay up a while longer and do some more work on the computer. If you don't mind, that is?"

"Of course not. It's your home. I mustn't forget to go to your little shop to get some honey before I go. I can't believe how quickly the week's gone."

"It has simply sped by. It's been great having you here. Can't you stay on a while longer?"

She laughed.

"I've almost run out of clean clothes."

"If that's the only reason, use the washer. Please stay on for a while longer. You haven't got to get back for work, after all."

"Let me think about it. I must call Emily and see how she's getting on. I'm going up to bed now. I promise, I will think about it."

"I'll let you off with that. Good night, love."

He rose and, as she got up, he leaned forward to kiss her.

"Sorry. I didn't mean to do that."

"It's all right," she whispered. "But I'm still going up to bed."

Shock Encounter

CAROLYN lay in bed and found she was shivering. It was ridiculous. She wasn't cold at all… It must be because Jed had kissed her. She had to admit, she had rather liked it. But then, she was so confused by her feelings…

She really must stop feeling so guilty. She assumed Henry wasn't feeling guilty in any way. Jed, she knew, was footloose and fancy free. Maybe he was falling for her, too. Her shivering increased and she sat up. This was quite silly, she realised. She grabbed her dressing gown and went downstairs again. Jed looked up.

"What's up?" he asked.

"I don't know. I suppose you had some sort of effect on me."

"I did say I was sorry," he told her. "You just looked so lovely and we'd had such a good time together."

"Whatever it was, it has stopped me from sleeping. Maybe I'm starting to get over what Henry did to me."

"That's good. I knew that a spell of concentrated Jed might be good for you. My own brand of special therapy. Works wonders, you know."

"I wanted to say, well… thank you. Thank you for being so patient with me. I can't be the easiest person to put up with."

"Nonsense. You've been great to have around. I'm desperately trying to control myself," he added.

"Really? You do surprise me. Does this mean... well, that you like me?"

"Like you? Of course I like you. So much that I'm prepared to wait till you're ready to consider... well to think about having someone else in your life."

He paused there and looked at her carefully, as if trying to assess the effect his words were having on her. She smiled at him and he immediately felt more confident.

"I know it's still too soon for you to make any sort of commitment but I want you to know I'm here for you – waiting for the time."

"Oh, Jed. You're very kind. I'm sorry to be such a wimp but I'm still a bit... wobbly."

"I know, love. As I say, I'm here for you. But just don't leave it too long, will you?"

She leaned over and kissed him, very gently.

"I'll remember what you said and I promise I won't leave you hanging on for too long. I'll let you know one way or the other quite soon. And yes please, I would like to stay on a while longer. Assuming you do indeed have a working washing machine."

"That's terrific. Do you want to put your washing in now?" He leaped off his seat and went towards the kitchen.

She laughed.

"Tomorrow will be fine. I'll sort it out in the morning."

Carolyn ran upstairs and settled down. She fell asleep quickly, smiling to herself. Jed came up some time later and with a sigh, went to his own room. He lay awake for ages, thinking about his future and would it actually include this woman who had made such an impact on him. Perhaps it was almost time to try a different tactic.

* * * *

The next morning, Carolyn came down with a large bundle of washing. She stuffed it all into the machine and stared at the control panel. It was a different machine to her own at home and she scratched her head, wondering what to do next. She decided to wait till Jed got here and let him sort it out.

She made some coffee and opened the back door, planning to take it outside. It started to rain. She cursed. Her washing was going to stay wet if she couldn't hang it out. Still, it was the first rain they'd had all week so she couldn't really complain. She went back into the lounge and put the television on. It was almost nine by the time her host arrived.

"Sorry," he said. "Didn't sleep all that well. Must have drifted off in the small hours and then slept through. How are you?"

"I'm fine, thanks. I've put my washing in the machine but wasn't sure which programme to use."

"I'll see to it. More coffee?"

"I can come and do it," she protested. "I don't expect you to do everything for me."

"Don't worry about it. Stay where you are and I'll do it. More coffee, as I asked before?"

"I'll come and sort out some breakfast. I wasn't really watching the television. It was just on."

"Anything new happening in the big wide world?"

"Just the usual stuff." She followed him into the kitchen and sorted their breakfast. "We're nearly out of honey. Shall we go and get some more? It's raining so maybe some shopping might be good."

"I'll take you to my little shop. It's only a

small place and a bit off the beaten track. They specialise in local products."

"Do they do pasties? I think it's about time we had more of them."

He laughed.

"Good. Got you hooked on the local food, have we? Yes, they do pasties."

"Great. And no arguing, I'm paying today."

"OK, fine. I've always wanted to be a kept man. You can buy two pasties."

"I'm not sure what I shall do with heaps of wet washing. It's raining, as I said."

"Not a problem. I have a tumble dryer. I was never prepared to festoon the place with wet washing. It's out in the garage."

They set off for the little shop he'd talked about. They both got out of his car and went inside.

"The honey's over here," Jed said.

But Carolyn was standing transfixed, staring at the man who was sitting by the till. He was equally transfixed as he gazed back at her.

"Henry!" she gasped.

"Carolyn! What on earth are you doing here?"

"I could ask you the same question."

"I work here."

"For how long? I mean, why? Why aren't you working with computers?"

"I like it here."

She felt weak at the knees and wondered how long she might remain standing. Her head buzzed and she thought she was about to faint.

Jed came up to her and took her arm. She looked round at him, grateful for his intervention.

"I take it you two know each other?" he asked.

"This is Henry. My... well, I suppose he's my ex."

Jed regarded Henry steadily.

"I'm Jed. Look, shall I leave you two alone for a while? You clearly have a lot to talk about." He swung round and went out of the shop.

The two looked at each other, their feelings in turmoil.

"How come...?" they both said at the same time.

"Sorry, you go on," Carolyn said.

"I drove down here after the... well, when we didn't get married. I'm so sorry. But I had to get as far away as possible, for your sake. I didn't want you to be harmed."

"Oh, no, of course not. You could do that by yourself, couldn't you? How could you do it to me? To all our guests?"

"I'm sorry. It was the only thing I could do. You really don't know the whole story. It's possibly better if you don't. They might still come after you."

"Who might? What are you talking about? You're not making any sense."

Henry certainly did look somewhat disturbed. Why on earth had he left like that?

"You need to tell me why you left me standing in my wedding dress when I was about to commit to you for ever."

"I can't. Believe me, I never wanted to hurt you."

"Huh!" She shook her head. "Well, you didn't succeed. I was desperately hurt. I'll never forgive you, ever."

"I deserve that."

She looked away from him and tried very hard to decide what to do next.

Just then, another customer came into the shop.

"Morning," the woman said. "I want some biscuits. Got a friend coming round for tea." She went round the side of the shop and picked up what she wanted.

"Disappointing weather today, isn't it?" she remarked to Carolyn as she brought her purchase to the till.

Carolyn nodded and watched as the woman paid and left.

"I'd never have seen you as a shop worker," Carolyn said to Henry.

"I've quite enjoyed the change. No real worries and responsibilities. And nobody to try to get you to do things..." He stopped at that point.

"What do you mean by that?"

"I don't want to talk about it."

"Come on. You didn't mean me, did you? The whole wedding thing – well, it was your idea. Remember? 'Let's get married,' you said. 'Let's make it soon.' You said you wanted to marry me. I didn't ask you. It was all down to you." She spoke in short sentences, her emotions starting to rise to the surface and threatening to take her over. He must give her some answers.

"I'm sorry. But you don't know the whole story. I still can't tell you everything."

"You're making no sense at all."

She looked into his eyes, as if trying to read into his soul. How could someone who had declared his undying love for her... how could he have done what he did?

"Can we start again? If you moved down here, perhaps we could begin our lives over," he suggested tentatively.

"No! Not for anything would I ever commit to you again. In fact, I think you did me a favour. If we had got married, it would probably never have worked out. When I think about it, I can see we weren't really suited. You were much too controlling about my life. Then it would have been a whole lot more complicated to separate."

"I can see you've moved on. This Jed character is now in your life. Well, good luck to you."

"He's a very good friend. He's been marvellous to me. Very kind and understanding. And, no, there's nothing else going on, before you accuse me of it. I still don't know why you ran away. Someone said they saw two rough-looking types hanging round before the wedding. Were they anything to do with you?"

"They might have been. They didn't get close to you?" he asked suddenly.

"I didn't see them. Just something someone said. So, who were they?"

"Some nasty types you don't want to know about. Look, it's about time I put the kettle on. Do you want some coffee?"

"No, thank you. Jed is still out there waiting for me."

****

Henry scowled. Was he jealous of the man and his ease at being with Carolyn.

"No, you mustn't upset Jed, of course not."

He sounded bitter, he knew, and it was all his own doing. He had dumped her and she had moved on.

"We came in to get some honey. Perhaps I'd better get it and go."

"Where are you staying?"

"With Jed. He's got a cottage about five miles from here."

"I've met him before. He's been in the shop to buy honey a few times. I suppose he seems a nice enough chap. Look, would you like to go out for a drink one night?"

"I don't think so. Besides, I'm supposed to be going home soon. It would be very awkward. And I don't have a car. Mine got stolen and torched."

"What? From outside the flat?"

"No, I was at Paul's place. It was taken from there. It means I don't have transport. I'm not sure I even want to see you again. You can't give me a reason for your actions so I think it's time to say goodbye."

"Please, Carolyn," Henry began. "Please don't treat me this way. Remember all the good times we had? The places we went to? Let's have a drink and see if we can't patch things up in some way."

He realised he was desperately lonely. He'd been almost happily moving along his track, not allowing himself any opportunity of meeting people apart from in the shop and it had all come back to him.

He wanted more out of life. For heaven's

sake, he was still a young man with a lot of life ahead of him.

Surely he would be off the hook if he went back? He was no longer working at Phoenix so his tormentors' demands couldn't be met in any case. They were full of meaningless threats. What could they do to him now?

He stared at the woman he thought he had loved. That love could surely be rekindled?

****

"I'm sorry, Henry. For so many reasons, including self-preservation, I have to say no."

Carolyn now felt more in control of herself and able to speak without crying.

"I'll buy a couple of jars of honey and go. I wish you well and hope you'll be happy. Where is the honey?"

"Over there," he said pointing at the row of jars. "Make your choice."

She looked at the number of different types of honey and felt confused. One of them she thought she recognised, so she picked up two jars, paid for them and hurried out of the shop.

She stopped by Jed's car but there was no sign of him. The rain had stopped and he'd obviously gone for a walk. She looked round, wondering which way he might have gone.

She started to walk towards the sea, still clutching the two jars. She went back and tried the car door. It wasn't locked, so she put the honey down on the seat and started to walk along the road again.

She had almost reached the beach when she saw Jed walking back towards her. She looked hard at him. He was considerably taller than Henry – better looking, too. He had a much kinder face. His hair was as dark as Henry's was blond.

It was wrong to compare the two men but she couldn't help it. She felt Jed was open and honest while Henry left much to be desired. He still had told her nothing about his reasons for calling off their wedding.

"Hi," Jed called to her. "Have you finished?"

"Quite finished. I don't ever want to see him again."

"You're sure?"

"As sure as I'll ever be."

"Did he explain himself?"

"Not at all. He made one or two cryptic remarks about me getting harmed. I ask you! Who on earth was going to hurt me? I told him he was quite capable of doing that himself."

He took her hand and together, they walked back to the car. She pulled her hand away before they reached the car, in case Henry might be watching. No need to rub it in. He clearly hadn't got another woman around or he'd never have asked her to go out for a drink with him.

It all remained a mystery.

"I put the honey in the car. I saw it wasn't locked."

"Oh, you got some?"

"I'm not sure it was exactly the same as the stuff you'd got but I'm sure it can be changed if necessary."

He glanced at it.

"No. It isn't the same. I doubt you'd like this one as much. Shall I go and change it or will you?"

"You go, if you don't mind. I feel I've had my fill of Henry for one day."

Jed picked up the two jars and went into the shop. He went straight to the counter and asked if he could exchange it.

"Sorry," Henry said. "I can't. Not once it's been bought and paid for. The till, you know..."

"Oh, for goodness' sake. It's the same price. Surely you can change it?"

"The bar code is recorded. Sorry, mate."

"I'm not your mate and never will be. Not after what you did to Carolyn. You really are a nasty piece of work, aren't you?"

"You know nothing about it at all. I was only trying to protect her from... well, I've said enough."

"I'd like to take you outside and give you a good hiding, except it's not the sort of thing I ever do. Someone like Carolyn does not deserve to be treated like that. However, you probably did me a big favour. I've never met anyone quite like her and in time, I hope she will settle with me and forget the despicable way you treated her."

Jed picked up the two jars, put them back on the shelf and helped himself to two new jars.

"Thanks for your co-operation."

He swept out of the shop and left Henry standing by the counter looking totally flabbergasted.

"Any problems?" Carolyn asked.

"None at all. He was fine."

"Really?" she said.

"Really," he repeated.

Difficult Decisions

CAROLYN was silent as they drove home. Jed decided to leave her with her thoughts. He remembered he'd intended to go to Truro today but somehow, the events of the morning had put paid to his plans. He remembered they'd also planned to have pasties for lunch and his mind ran through what was in the fridge. Nothing.

"We forgot to buy pasties," he said.

"Oh, yes. I'm sorry."

"I also need to go to Truro today. You don't have to come if you'd prefer to stay at home. I can do some shopping there, too."

"No, it's all right. I will come. No point me sitting at home stewing, is there? Do you want to go straight there now?"

"I have to collect the stuff from home. And your washing will be finished by now. I'm not sure what to offer you to eat. I think we're pretty well out of most things."

They decided to go to Truro and buy pasties there. They stopped at the cottage, emptied out the washer and put it to tumble dry. Jed collected all the stuff for the printer and put it into a folder.

He turned to Carolyn.

"Right. I'm ready, if you are."

She nodded and they set off. She was still rather quiet and at last, Jed asked her if she wanted to talk about it.

"I think I'm still confused. I mean, how can Henry possibly sit in that little shop all day and serve customers? He was always such a whizz kid with computers. He could make them do things that made my mind boggle. Now he's given it all up and is in a shop."

"There's nothing wrong with being a shopkeeper. Perhaps he likes not having the pressure of a job where he's under pressure all the time. I told you, I was working for a company like that. I came down here and took up my favourite hobby. Luckily for me, it's worked and brings me a reasonable income. Enough for me, anyway. And some left over for anyone to share it with me."

He looked hard at her, wondering what she would make of his remark but her face was expressionless.

****

They reached Truro and found a parking space in one of the multi-storey car parks.

"That was easy," she remarked. "I was expecting to be driving round for hours looking for somewhere to stop."

"It's a bit late for the early shoppers so we're in luck. I'll call in at the printers and then we'll find some pasties. There's a shop that sells lovely ones near the Panier Market. That's a big indoor market, in case you're wondering."

She followed him through the cobbled streets and looked at some of the shops as they passed them. Somehow, shopping didn't really appeal to her. She had a whole lot of new clothes bought for the honeymoon that never was and she couldn't face even looking at them. She was happiest in her shirts and jeans.

She didn't even have a job anymore, so her working clothes were now also redundant. Still, she would have to look for another job, so perhaps then they'd come back into use.

They reached the printers and Jed leaped into action, describing exactly how he wanted the brochures printed. He started negotiating the price. Carolyn smiled at his professional ease. He knew exactly how difficult the job was and how much time they'd need to spend on it. They reached a deal and he shook hands with the printer.

"I'll collect them on Monday, shall I?"

"Best give us till Tuesday. We have a couple of urgent deadlines to meet."

"All right. Tuesday it is. Is that all right

with you, Carolyn?"

"Of course. Why wouldn't it be?"

"I was thinking you needed to go back."

"I hadn't thought that far ahead. If you're willing to put up with me, that's fine."

"OK. I'll see you on Tuesday. Call me if there's any change." They left the print shop and walked back the way they'd come. "Pasties next. You still want one?"

"Mmm. Can we sit out on the big square to eat them?"

"The Piazza, you mean?"

"Whatever it's called. We can watch people go by. I love people watching, don't you?"

"Of course. Only trouble is, I want to photograph them as they go by. Not many people allow that sort of behaviour."

"Maybe they have guilty consciences. Don't want to be seen here or with someone they want kept secret."

"You have a good imagination. I suspect it's more likely they feel scruffy and not ready to be photographed. It's over here, the pasty shop."

Soon they were sitting eating, along with several other people.

"That was scrumptious," she said as she ate the last bit of her pasty.

"You've got bits of pastry on your jacket. Here, let me brush them off." He leaned over and brushed them away. "You all right?"

"I think so. Yes, of course I am. Why wouldn't I be? In Truro with a good-looking, talented man and I've just eaten a pasty."

"That's OK, then. Good-looking?" he queried, looking round. "You must introduce me sometime. I'm sitting with a very beautiful young lady who could have any man she wanted."

"Oh, yes? I didn't do very well so far, did I?"

"Depends on what you want out of life."

"Well, thank you for the compliment anyway. So, what's next? Supermarket?"

He nodded and got up from his seat. They went back to his car and drove round to the supermarket. They didn't take long to collect all they needed and they were soon on the way back home.

"I would love a walk down to the beach after we've unpacked the shopping. I don't mind going on my own, if you like."

"Sounds like a good idea. I'd like to come with you unless you need to be alone. After this morning's encounter, I mean."

She shook her head.

"I feel very calm about seeing him again. I really think I've moved on. It's less than two months since the wedding that never was. I think a lot of that is down to you, actually."

"I'm very glad. You... well, you must realise you've come to mean a lot to me?"

"So you've told me," she said gently. "But it's still much too soon for me to be involved with anyone again. I'm sorry but I must be damaged goods. Secondhand Rose, that's me."

She looked through the car window as she was speaking, hoping to hide from him the tears that were pricking at the back of her eyes. Fortunately, even if he did see, he said nothing. She wondered what it must have cost him to make those comments to her. Perhaps one day, if he was prepared to wait, they might even make a go of it.

"Here we are. Home again. You OK?"

"Yes. I'll grab these bags, shall I?"

They walked up the path and he unlocked the cottage door and picked up a pile of letters from the mat. They both went into the kitchen and began to put away the shopping.

He put the kettle on to make some tea and her mobile phone rang. She looked at the number but it wasn't a familiar one.

"Hello?" she said hesitantly.

"Carolyn. It's me. Henry."

"Henry. Why are you calling me? And where are you calling from?"

Jed left her and went into the garden, taking his letters with him.

"I'm calling from the shop. I had to speak to you. After I saw you today, well, I realised everything I've lost."

"It was your choice," she snapped.

"Not really. I was forced into a corner I couldn't get out of. Look, can we meet? I really need to explain things to you. Perhaps then we... well, perhaps we could –"

"I don't think that's a good idea. I'm sorry but no. I really can't."

"Is that anything to do with the chap you were with?"

"That's really none of your business but, as I told you before, he's a very good friend who is helping me to... well, to come to terms with my life."

"How long do you intend to stay in Cornwall?"

"I shall be going back soon."

"I take it you've taken time off work. How is that, by the way?"

"It's rather quiet at the moment. Well, actually, it's all burned down. I'm not sure where we're going from here. Emily is having a bit of a trauma."

"Goodness! I am sorry. Sorry, I've got to go. I'll call you tomorrow. And please, let me see you again. Just coming, Mrs..." The line went dead.

Carolyn went outside to look for Jed. He was sitting looking somewhat pensive.

"You all right?" he asked. "Are you going to see him again?"

"No. He asked me to but I've said no."

"Up to you, of course. Maybe you would have heard why he decided to leave you."

"He was a bit cryptic. Said it was for my sake, or some such drivel. How on earth can I believe that? He says he'll phone me again tomorrow but he was interrupted before I could tell him not to."

Jed was quiet for a few moments, giving her time to think.

"Did you want some tea?"

"Oh, yes, please."

"I'll make it. The kettle boiled but I left you to your call. Won't be a minute."

She saw a couple of letters lying beside his seat. He'd obviously been reading them when she came out. He handed her a mug of tea and sat down again without speaking. After a few minutes, he said, "I've had a letter from the solicitors of the chap who owns this place. Evidently, he's decided to sell it. He's given me first option on it."

"And will you buy it?"

"I very much doubt I could afford it. I told you it was falling apart when I came in. He's now put it on the market at a ridiculous price. Oh, it may be worth it in a way but I really feel cross he isn't allowing me anything for all the work I did."

"That's terrible," Carolyn sympathised.

"He paid for the larger things like the bathroom suite and he also paid for the kitchen units but I fitted them all. I did all the painting and decorating. And I renewed the plaster where it was needed. I did no end of stuff to improve the place. It would have cost him a fortune to get someone else to do it."

"So what will you do?" Carolyn had forgotten her own worries for the time being. "Will you make him an offer?"

"I don't think he'll even listen to me. Admittedly, I've had a cheap rental from him for a year or two but that was because I was working on the place. It seems he now wants to make his money and get me out."

"But where would you live? I mean, if this place is sold, that means you'll have to start over again. Can't you afford to even consider it?"

"Not at his inflated prices. I suppose it will be a case of starting over."

"Like me, you mean. I've got to face that too. At least I own my flat outright. My parents left me enough money to buy it and have some left over. Paul is the same, of course. He owns his place."

"Then you're both quite lucky. I've never

had a great deal of savings and when I came down here, I used most of them up before my business took off. Not much of a catch, am I?"

She smiled at him, thinking he was actually quite a catch for someone. He was so good-looking and seemed to have such a lovely personality, she could almost fall for him herself.

She looked away, thinking she was quite stupid. She was still trying to get over Henry, wasn't she? Not helped by having seen him only that morning and hearing him on the phone so recently.

But no, she was not going there again. She had been well and truly hurt by him and would never risk it again. Still, Jed seemed different. So caring and thoughtful in ways that Henry had never been.

"You didn't reply to my comment. You were supposed to argue like mad and say I am a good catch."

"I was thinking about it. Of course you are. You're lovely – and very good looking. There, that has to be enough for now."

"Thank you. All the same, it looks as though I can't afford to stay in my lovely cottage. I really don't know where I should go next."

"I'm sorry. Surely you could get a mortgage? All this stuff in the news about help to buy, you know?"

"I've never given it much thought. Besides, although I make a reasonable living, I don't have a regular income. Well, not something I could write down and say this is my annual income. Nor do I have much of a deposit."

"I think you should try for it. Speak to the farmer or whoever it is who owns the place and tell him what you've told me. He may listen. If you don't even try, you're just rolling over on your back and waving your legs in the air."

He laughed.

"Nice picture you paint. I'll think about it. But what about you? What are you going to do?"

"I don't think I want to see Henry again. Though I would like to know his reason for leaving the way he did and why he's being so mysterious about it."

"Then do go to meet him. You can take my car."

"You wouldn't consider coming with me, I suppose?"

He looked shocked.

"I don't think it's my place. It's something you have to do on your own, I'm afraid."

"I'll think about it. Is there any more tea in that pot?"

He poured a cup for her and they sat in

companionable silence, each one busy with their own thoughts.

Jed was mentally going through his finances. He wondered how much he'd have to pay as a deposit and how much he'd have to borrow. The figures were daunting. He felt he was a good bet for repayments but would anyone else believe him?

Carolyn was thinking about Henry. She knew he would try to persuade her to go back to him. She didn't feel she even wanted to go and see him. He was good-looking in his way but even his looks seemed to have faded somewhat.

He'd lost some of his confidence. In fact, he seemed to have lost most of it. What had happened to him? Why on earth was he working in a shop? With his qualifications and previous experience, he was surely crazy to throw all that away? Perhaps she should go and see him again and find out what was going on...

"I think perhaps I should go and meet Henry," she announced at last.

"Good. I think you should."

"I can't persuade you to come?" she almost begged him.

"No. You need to do this on your own."

"But suppose he tries to persuade me to go back to him?"

"You have to follow your heart. I may not like it but you must do whatever you think is the right thing. Borrow my car. I really don't mind."

"Thank you. If you're sure. I'm not sure where he'll want to meet but he's going to phone me later."

"Fine. I'll go and get something ready for our supper."

"I'll come and help. And Jed, thank you very much."

"Whatever for?"

"For being so understanding."

He didn't reply but looked away. He was beginning to realise what he'd done. He was offering her his car to go and meet her ex-fiancé and possibly to get back together with him. How would he feel about that?

Gutted, was his first thought. He would have to hope that Carolyn was sensible, if that was the right word. He couldn't say anything to express how he was feeling.

****

"What do you fancy for supper?" he muttered.

"Don't mind."

"One of my concoctions it is, then." He looked into the fridge and dragged out a pack of mince. "Do you fancy chopping some onions? I'll make a spaghetti something or other."

"OK. Are you all right, Jed? Only you seem a bit quiet. Quieter than usual." He was concentrating on making his sauce and she felt concerned.

"I'm fine, thanks. Making a sauce." He went quiet again and she looked at him anxiously.

"I haven't said I will see Henry again. Not yet, anyway."

He gave a start.

"You should see him if you want to. Don't mind me."

"Actually, I do mind about you."

There, she'd said it. Not quite sure why, but she had said it.

He stopped what he was doing and stared at her.

"I'm glad about that. Very glad, but you do have unfinished business with Henry. I'd feel better if you wouldn't be tempted to go back to him but I also feel you need to know why he did what he did."

"Oh, Jed, I wouldn't go back to him. But you're right, I do need some answers. I need to understand why he rushed away and why he's now working down here. You must admit, it is a coincidence."

"Of all the bars in all the world, sort of coincidence, you mean?"

"Well, yes. I find it amazing that he should have come down here."

"Maybe he had childhood holidays down here."

"Maybe. He never mentioned it if he did. Are these onions chopped finely enough?"

"They'll do. Can you open some tomatoes? There are some cans in the cupboard. No, that one over the sink."

She did as she was told, still thinking hard about what she should do.

She watched this man stirring the pan of sauce. How did she really feel about him? How did he feel about her?

She knew she was attracted to him and after staying with him in his house for a few days, she had really felt at ease in his company. Could she live with him indefinitely? Maybe.

But then, she had felt that about Henry. She had been looking forward to their lives together. Now, she could see things had never been quite right but she had been willing to compromise and hope it would all work out. But Jed was quite a different prospect.

Words Of Love

JED and Carolyn ate a quiet supper, both of them feeling somewhat subdued. She had heard nothing more from Henry and hadn't really expected him to phone her again.

"I might turn in," Jed announced eventually. "I feel pretty bushed."

"I wouldn't mind an early night myself," she agreed. "You go and I'll clear up the supper things."

"If you're sure. Thanks. I'll go up and be out of your way in the bathroom."

"Night, Jed. Sleep well."

"You too." He went up the narrow stairs and she heard him running the water and then his bedroom door shutting.

After she'd washed up their few supper things and dried them, she opened the back door and stood looking at the moon. It was almost full and shone out brightly over the garden. She stepped outside, thinking how beautiful a place this was. The roses were all well open and produced a heavenly scent.

She slumped down on one of the seats and thought about life, her own in particular. What was she going to do now the company had burned down? She really must phone Emily and see how she was.

She sat for a while longer and finally rose and went inside, her mind still running round in circles. How on earth she would sleep, she had no idea.

An hour later, she was lying in bed, still wide awake. She decided to go down and get a drink of water and see if she could find something to read. Jed must have something she might like.

She went downstairs and poured herself a glass of water then went into the lounge and looked along his bookshelf. She saw several things she had already read and was surprised to find they shared a liking for a number of the same authors. She picked up an old favourite and carried it back to her room.

"Can't you sleep, either?" Jed asked, popping his head round the door of his room as she was crossing the landing.

She jumped and replied, "Not really. I wasn't as tired as I thought I was. I sat out in the garden for a while. I've borrowed one of your books. I hope you don't mind."

"Of course not. I was going to make some tea. Do you want some?"

"I suppose it may be better than water. I'll come down with you."

It was almost midnight and they went to sit in the comfortable seats in the lounge.

Jed sipped his tea and at last he spoke.

"Carolyn, I've been thinking... about Henry and you. Don't say anything till I've spoken, please. I said I didn't mind you seeing him again. That's not strictly true."

"But..."

"No, wait. Let me have my say. I've thought long and hard and I've realised I really don't want you to see him again. I'm scared. Scared of losing you. I know we don't have any sort of commitment to each other but I'd like there to be. Well, some sort of commitment anyway...

"You see, I've fallen in love with you. I know we haven't known each other for very long but I also know it's genuine love that I feel. There, I've said it now."

She stared at him, her mouth falling slightly open.

"Well, go on, say something," he urged.

"I don't know what to say." Carolyn was still trying to take in his words.

"Tell me I'm crazy if you must. Better still, tell me you care just a little for me."

"Oh, Jed. Of course I care for you. I'm still just wondering if it isn't a bit too soon. After Henry, I mean."

He looked positively crestfallen. As if his world was coming to an end.

"I'm sorry," she added. "I do really care and when a decent amount of time has gone by, I'm probably going to say I love you, too."

"I suppose if that's the best you can do, I'll have to put up with that. I'm just afraid that if you go back or if you see Henry again, he'll persuade you to return to him. I couldn't bear that."

"I'm not likely to go back to him. Whatever he says to me, I won't go back. But you must realise everything I own is back in Buckinghamshire. My friends and family are all there. My work is there. Or rather it was. I need to call Emily tomorrow and see what she's planning to do. You do understand, don't you, love?"

"I suppose so. You can't blame me for feeling disappointed, though. Somehow, I'd hoped for more. Forget what I said anyway. I'm going back to bed now." He rose and went back to his room, leaving her sitting on the sofa, feeling even more confused.

"Oh, Jed," she whispered. She too rose and went back to her room. This time, she fell asleep quickly.

****

They were both asleep till after nine the next morning. Carolyn staggered downstairs feeling rather groggy. She reached for the kettle and filled it. She really needed coffee. Jed arrived down as the kettle boiled.

"Coffee?" she asked.

"Please. I didn't sleep much, did you?"

"I did, actually, but I can't say my mind is any clearer today."

"I meant what I said. I'm not hurrying you but you needed to know how I was feeling. Have you any more thoughts?"

"I... I'm not sure I can talk about our future just yet. So much is up in the air. It's not that long since I was dumped at the altar, don't forget." She looked away, feeling slightly guilty that she had even thought about this man in terms of a long relationship. "I'm going to phone Emily shortly. I need to know what she's going to do about the company."

"To see if you still have a job, you mean?"

"Well, yes. It's a case of will she rebuild the office or not."

"And if she doesn't? What will you do then?"

"I just have no idea. Maybe I can get something else with another company. Or perhaps I should change my career totally. Be a shop girl," she added wryly.

"You could always come and work for me."

"Oh yes? Doing what exactly?"

"I mentioned I was thinking of opening a shop or gallery. You could help me with pictures, too. I don't know. Loads of things."

"I'll add it to my list of things to think about. Have you thought any more about buying this place?"

"I've thought about it. I doubt whether anyone would lend me the money. Oh, I've no doubt I could pay it back but my earnings are pretty erratic. I can earn a small fortune one month and then go for two or three with low wages. It depends if the mortgage people see me as a safe bet."

"Then you should find out. Make an appointment to see someone."

"You reckon?"

"Certainly. Go for it."

"OK, I will. Bank, do you think?"

"Give them a try first of all."

They had both finished their coffee and Jed made some toast. They ate in silence, each busy with their own thoughts.

When she had finished, Carolyn said she was going to speak to Emily. She dialled her number and waited. At last a somewhat sleepy sounding voice answered.

"Hello?"

"It's Carolyn. I wondered how you are and whether you've made any plans yet?"

"Carolyn? Oh, Carolyn. No dear. No

plans." Emily sounded weary.

"So what are you going to do about the company? I mean, do I still have a job?"

"A job? What sort of job?"

"Emily, are you all right? You sound very strange."

"I'm feeling rather unwell. Sorry, dear, I have to go now." With that, she hung up.

"Goodness, she sounded in a terrible state. I really think I should go back," Carolyn said to Jed as she returned to the kitchen.

"Really? What can you do?"

"I don't know. But she sounded so bad. She could barely speak to me."

"Isn't there someone else you could speak to? Someone who could go to see her?"

"I suppose so. I'll call Sophie. She's one of our secretaries." She scrolled down her contacts and punched in Sophie's number.

"Sophie? It's Carolyn. I wondered if you've been in touch with Emily?"

"I tried but she wouldn't speak to me. Why?"

"I just called her and she seemed very strange. I wondered if you could go and see her? And call me back?"

"I suppose I could. I'm going for an interview today but I could go round later."

"An interview? Where?"

"Just another company in the town. I

didn't think anything was going to happen with Emily. I mean, she hasn't done anything about the company, has she?"

"I don't know – that's why I was ringing her. You've got my mobile number. If you can call round to see her and find out anything, let me know."

"OK. I must say, I'm disappointed to lose the job with her company. Can't afford not to work, though, hence my interview."

"OK. 'Bye for now." Carolyn frowned. "Maybe I'll wait to see if she finds out anything and then consider what I'm going to do."

"I'll take you back, of course, if that's what you want," Jed offered. "I'll put my problems on hold for a while."

"That's good of you. But I can easily get a train. I don't want to drag you all that way."

"Nonsense. Of course I'll take you. Let's wait to see what Sophie says."

****

It was a slightly edgy day for both of them. At about three o'clock, the printers rang to tell Jed that the brochures were ready.

"I think I'll go and fetch them. Then if we do go back to your place tomorrow, it won't be a hold up."

"Can I come with you?" Carolyn asked. "If I take my mobile with me, I won't miss a call from Sophie."

"Right, then, Truro here we come. I wondered about taking the brochures round to Mrs James afterwards."

"Fine by me. It'll mean we're both free tomorrow."

They drove to Truro and collected the brochures. They did look wonderful and Jed paid for them happily. He felt cheerful as they drove towards Penzance and the holiday complex.

"I'll keep a few back as advertising material," he said. "Always good to have some of my own products to show people."

Carolyn's phone rang and she answered it quickly.

"Hi, it's me. Just got a quiet moment in the shop."

"Henry," she mouthed to Jed. "Hello, Henry."

"I'd like to see you this evening. Please say you will meet me. Or I can come and pick you up from wherever you are."

"I'm not sure..." she hesitated.

"Please, darling Carolyn. Please come to see me."

"I may be going back tomorrow. I'm not sure yet."

"Just one drink. I really need to explain

myself to you."

"One drink, then. Where do you want to meet?"

"Do you know the Fisherman's Cove? It's a pub down by the coast."

"Fisherman's Cove," she repeated for Jed's benefit. He nodded. "All right. About nine o'clock. I'll see you then."

"That's great. Thank you so much. I know it's going to be all right. We'll soon be sorted and back to normal." He put down the phone before she could say anything else.

"He's definitely in organising mode. He seems to think one drink and I'll run back to him. Please won't you come along?"

"I could come and sit in one of the other rooms, if you really want me to."

"Yes, please. I'd really appreciate that. Just knowing you're nearby will make all the difference."

"Hey, come on, love. It's only a drink with your ex-fiancé."

"That's not what you said last night."

"Last night was last night. I was probably being over-emotional. In the cold light of day, it all seems so much clearer. I love you. You don't seem to love me. I'll get over it."

"I never said I didn't. I'm still emotional over being dumped. A bit scared of getting dumped again."

He stopped the car in the next lay-by.

"Carolyn, please don't think like that. It was weird that he left you the way he did and clearly he had his reasons. But it was nothing to do with you. At least, that's the way I see it."

"All the same, it does hurt."

"I know, love. But don't think all men are the same. Some of us are quite reasonable guys – especially ones that are in love."

"You keep saying that."

"I want you to get used to the idea. Now, if we don't get on the road again, we'll never make it to the Fisherman's this evening."

Mrs James was absolutely thrilled with her brochures when she saw them in reality.

"They look marvellous," she told them. "You'll send me your bill, won't you?"

"Of course. I'm glad you like them. I'll finish your website along the same lines, shall I?"

"Yes, please. I really am delighted with your work, Jed. Let's have a drink to celebrate."

She went to the fridge and produced a bottle of dry white wine.

"Only a very small one for me. I'm driving," Jed told her.

"That's a pity. You could stay for supper with us."

"I'm sorry but we have an appointment later. But thanks very much for the offer."

"So, are you two... you know... together?" Mrs James couldn't resist asking the question and Carolyn felt herself blush.

"Not quite yet," Jed told her. "I have high hopes of persuading her, though."

Mrs James turned to Carolyn.

"Oh, I see. Playing hard to get, are you?" she teased.

"Not at all," Carolyn protested. "I just... well, I'm not quite ready to commit."

"I won't ask any more, my dear. I'm sure you have your reasons. But don't leave it too long or someone else will snap him up."

"Hey, I'm not some commodity to be snapped up, as you put it," Jed said indignantly.

They all laughed.

"I think we might need to get on our way," Jed said. "Thanks very much for the wine and sorry to be a bit negative about staying to eat with you."

"Perhaps we can arrange for you both to come on another evening." Mrs James smiled.

"That would be lovely, thank you," Carolyn said.

They drove back to Jed's cottage. The sky had clouded over and a few drops of rain began to fall.

"Looks like being a rather damp end to the day. Is that usual in Cornwall?"

"It does seem to rain quite a bit. But it's what makes everywhere so green."

It was raining heavily by the time they stopped. They both ran inside and got soaked on their way.

"Why now?" Carolyn wailed. "I'll have to change before we go out."

"What do you want to eat?" Jed asked.

"I think I'm too nervous to eat much. How about something simple like cheese on toast?"

"Cheese on toast?"

"I love cheese on toast. What's wrong with that?"

"Not exactly much of a main meal."

"Oh, do whatever you like. I'm going to change out of my wet things."

She ran upstairs and peeled of her soggy jeans. What should she wear? She really didn't want to look too dressed up but nor did she want to look scruffy.

She was half into a different pair of jeans when her mobile rang. It was Sophie.

"Hi, there. I went round to Emily's place. She's in a bad way. I suspect she'd been drinking heavily. Didn't want me to go inside her house but I persuaded her to allow me in. It really was a mess."

"Oh, poor woman. Could you get anything out of her? Re the business, I mean."

"Nothing. She isn't even thinking straight about her life. You know, I wondered if she may have set the fire herself? The business was well insured and she stands to get a good payment."

"Not if she started the fire, she won't."

"I don't mean she set a match to anything. Maybe she left something on that would overheat. An electric fire or something."

"Has she been questioned? By the police or anyone?"

"I couldn't tell. I suspect she may have been. I went past the old building. It's pretty much been demolished. Safety, I suspect."

"Well, thanks very much for going to see Emily. Please tell her I'll come and see her as soon as I get home. I'll probably come back in the next day or two. How did you get on with the interview, by the way?"

"I got it. Start next week."

"Well done. Congratulations."

"Thanks. I'll see you sometime. Mustn't lose touch."

Carolyn felt puzzled as she finished dressing. She did feel concerned for her old friend and colleague. In all honesty, Emily had been losing the plot lately. She had wondered if there was something wrong with her.

She went down to the kitchen where she smelled wonderful aromas.

"What are you making?"

"Wait and see. Did you get your call from Sophie?"

"Yes. It seems Emily was in a rather bad way. I would like to go back quite soon."

"Then so you shall, madame. Tomorrow or the next day?"

"Next day, I think. I may need to get over this evening and won't want to dash off right away."

"Sit down and eat. I've made you one of my special omelettes."

"You're very good to me."

"I know. I must be mad."

"Oh, Jed."

Magical Kisses

THEY set off for the pub at around eight-thirty. It was situated in a small village by the sea and the car park was fairly full.

"Anywhere left for you to park?" Carolyn asked.

"I'll have to leave it on the road a bit further way. You go on in and I'll see you later. Good luck."

"Thanks. I won't stay too long."

"No worries."

She got out of his car and watched as he drove away. She could so easily fall in love with him, she was thinking. She went inside and saw Henry immediately. It was a small bar and he was sitting at one side, a bottle of wine in front of him.

"Come and sit down. I got a bottle of your favourite wine. It's so good to see you again."

"Thank you. I did say one drink. I did mean that."

"It's only one bottle." He poured a large glass for her and handed it to her. He poured a smaller one for himself. "Here's to us."

She didn't raise her glass to that particular

toast. She was looking for Jed but he didn't come in. She sipped the wine.

"So what do you want to say?"

"First of all, I'm so sorry for leaving you the way I did. I really mean that. When I explain my reasons, I hope you'll forgive me."

"I can't think of any reason why I should."

"It was for your sake."

"My sake? How on earth can you say that?"

"There were these two ruffians. Really hard types. They threatened me if I didn't do as they wanted. They had a boss, and he wanted me to alter some stuff on the computer system. He wanted to make a lot of money out of it. When I said no, I couldn't do it, they threatened me – or rather, you. Said they'd probably kill you. Or implied it anyway."

Shocked by Henry's revelations, Carolyn demanded, "How on earth did you get involved with them in the first place?"

He looked away.

"They promised me a lot of money. Said it would be enough to buy a nice house. I really wanted to please you and so I initially agreed to their plan. Then when I saw exactly what they wanted, I backed off and said I couldn't. The two heavies turned up on the morning of the wedding and well, I ran for it."

"I see. But you must have known they were shady characters when you first met up with them."

"I was tempted by easy money."

"You really are an idiot. As if I ever cared about having a posh house. I love my flat. I'd never have been impressed by any of that."

"I hated living in a home that was all yours. I wanted independence. You must understand that."

"I suppose so."

"So, can we get back together? Please?"

"I'm sorry. I'm still fond of you but you behaved stupidly and left me almost at the altar. I really don't feel the same about you as I once did."

"It's that man you're living with, isn't it? You can't be so stupid, surely not. It's only five minutes since we were about to be married." His eyes had narrowed and he looked very angry.

"It's almost two months ago."

"Whatever. So, is it about him?"

"It's more about you. I really don't love you anymore. I'm sorry but I only feel relieved we didn't go through with it. It's taken me a while to get to feel like that."

"But we could get it back. I know we could."

"You might, but I won't. As I say, I'm sorry. Why are you working in that shop?"

"I just needed some sort of job. To pay my rent. It's a remarkably cheap and easy way to live. I like not having too many responsibilities. I do the shop's books for the owner. They're very easy to keep in order and she's quite elderly."

"That's nice of you. But surely you get bored silly?"

"I might do in the winter months when there's very little trade. But I was hoping that might be something I wouldn't have to contend with. Please think about us getting back together. We could sell your flat and find somewhere completely different."

"I'm sorry, Henry. You know my answer. I wish you well and hope you can be happy again at some point. I'm actually going back home tomorrow or maybe the next day."

"Can I ring you there? I can't use my mobile in case it can be traced. I know I should get a new one – I just haven't got round to it."

Carolyn nodded.

"It's almost shocking how you can be traced to any point anywhere simply by using your mobile phone. Anyway, I really must be going now."

"But there's still a lot of wine left. Do have another."

"I've had enough, thank you. Perhaps you could take it home with you. I did say one drink anyway."

She gathered up her things.

"I don't want an argument so I'm going to leave now. Goodbye, Henry. Good luck."

"I wish you meant that," he snarled, downing his own glass and pouring out more. "Looks as if I'll have to finish the bottle all by myself. Have a nice life."

He turned away and seemed to concentrate on his glass.

She sighed and left him. She hoped Jed was waiting for her in another room. She looked around outside to see if there was another entrance, leading to another room.

But then she spotted him, sitting on the sea wall, staring out to sea. He looked lost in thought and a little bit sad.

"Penny for them," she said coming up behind him.

"Just wondering how you were getting on. What did he say?"

"I'll tell you on the way home. Let's get away now, before he comes out and follows us."

"It was that bad, was it?"

"He was all right. Got a bit sour at the end when I said I wouldn't go back to him. The end of an era."

Jed caught her hand as they walked back

to the car. She felt grateful to him for not pestering about what Henry had said.

She felt suddenly drained and somewhat emotional. It wouldn't take much for her to cry and she swallowed hard, not wanting to break down. She sat quietly in his car as they drove back to his cottage. He showed tremendous patience with her and said nothing.

"Do you want some coffee or tea?"

"You haven't got any chocolate, have you? I need a chocolate fix."

"A drink, do you mean?"

"That'll do it."

He soon came back with two large mugs of chocolate.

"There you are, Carolyn. Enjoy."

"I should tell you about Henry's reason for running away."

"Only when you're ready. You don't have to."

She told him what Henry had said. He made no comment and listened carefully.

"And how do you feel about that?"

"Just how stupid he was. I really don't know why he thought he could impress me with money. I told him I was perfectly happy with my flat. Silly man."

"So, will you see him again?"

"I hope not. I just think it's better to leave it all in the past now. Oh, I can still remember some good times but it was all a bit superficial."

She shook her head.

"Thinking it over, he loved money and was ready to splash it around. We were always going out places for meals and he would invite a group of people to go with us. I enjoyed it at the time but now, it doesn't seem right. I'm much happier here, with you."

He blushed slightly.

"Does this mean you think we may have some sort of future together?"

"Don't rush me, please. As Henry pointed out, it wasn't that long since he and I were getting married."

"Sorry. But I needed to know."

"I think so. A definite maybe," she joked.

"OK. Enough said."

All the same, Jed looked like the proverbial cat sitting in front of a pot of cream.

"I've finished my chocolate now. Thank you for that. I think it's way past my bedtime."

"Off you go, then. I'll be up later. Are we going back tomorrow?"

"Can I decide in the morning? I feel absolutely worn out now. Can't make a sensible decision at this time of night."

As Carolyn went upstairs and got ready for bed, she thought about the evening.

Henry really was now in the past. When she had come out of the pub and seen Jed sitting on the sea wall, she had known. She had felt so much relief seeing him.

But somehow, she still felt it was all too soon. Rebound was the word that sprung into her mind. All the same, she didn't want to lose Jed by procrastinating for too long.

She tried to remember what he had said about his own life. What was the expression he had used? He was allergic to marriage? He seemed to have changed his views somewhat.

She finished brushing her teeth and went through to her room. Though she felt exhausted, she couldn't fall asleep. Her mind was racing through the events of the day. Emily, Truro, then Mrs James and finally meeting Henry.

"Go away, all of you," she muttered and turned over once more.

This time she did go to sleep and was troubled by dreams that caused her to wake several times.

* * * *

"Wake up, sleepyhead," Jed said, coming in to the bedroom with a cup of tea without milk, just how she liked it. "I nearly came in earlier but decided you wouldn't appreciate being woken."

"What time is it?"

"Half past nine."

"Oh, goodness!"

"Doesn't matter. I was wondering how you feel about going back home?"

"Not mad keen but maybe we should."

"We could have a day on the beach and go tomorrow. It's a lovely day after the rain. Pity to leave it all behind but we can go if you want to."

"You've persuaded me. Beach it is today and we'll go tomorrow. Make an early start?"

"If that suits, ma'am. You do look lovely when you wake up."

"I don't believe you. I look a wreck this morning."

"You look tousled and still pretty sleepy. Do you want to sleep on a bit?"

"Tempting. But no, I'll finish the tea and then get up. We shouldn't waste too much of the day. There are good beaches waiting for us to go to them. Can we have pasties again? I really like them."

"Presumably not from Henry's shop?"

"Oh. I forgot about that."

"We'll go to another beach and find some on the way. There's a wonderful place about six miles away, where they bake them on site. They're usually very hot, fresh out of the oven. We'll buy them and then eat them later on the beach. How does that sound?"

"Wonderful. Go away now and let me get up."

"Don't be too long. I've got breakfast all ready for you."

"What a wonderful man you are."

"Yes, well, don't you forget it."

He shot off downstairs again and she stretched out, luxuriating in a lazy day ahead with nothing much to do except enjoy it. She could smell bacon cooking. She rarely ate bacon but it really smelled so good she had a shower, dressed quickly and almost ran down the stairs.

"That smells wonderful."

"Thought it might get you down. Go on out into the garden. I'll bring out the breakfast."

"What luxury," she told him.

She went and sat at the little table and waited. He soon came out with a large tray with coffee and toast and two plates of bacon and eggs.

"Tuck in," he instructed.

When they had finished, she sat back feeling very content.

"That was a lovely breakfast. Thank you very much."

"My pleasure. I enjoyed it, too. Now, let's

wash up and get going. Do you like surfing?"

"Surfing? I've never tried it."

"Then we shall go to a surfing beach. We'll hire a couple of boards and you can have a lesson."

"I'm not sure I'd be any good. But I'll give it a try. I suppose you need good balance."

"Well, yes. But that's when you try to stand. You need to do some body boarding first. That's pretty easy and you get a sense of finding the waves." He was obviously quite keen and probably a good surfer.

"I'm not really sure. I'll happily come and watch you if you want to go."

"Bring your swimming things anyway and decide later. We'll still go to the surfing beach. I bet you won't be able to resist." She said nothing and just looked at him quizzically.

They called for pasties en route to the beach and their aroma filled the car.

"If I wasn't still full of breakfast, I'd eat mine right now," she muttered.

"Then you wouldn't have it to eat on the beach. And you did say that was where you wanted to eat it."

It was a beautiful day and the beach he'd chosen was indeed lovely. She did go into the sea and took a board with her. She enjoyed the experience but felt it would be a long time before she would ever be able to stand up like the experts.

It was late afternoon before they set off back to Jed's cottage. When they got back, Jed discovered several messages on the phone from his landlord. He was complaining that someone wanted to visit the place with a prospect of buying it and he couldn't let them in.

Jed frowned.

"Now what do I do? I really don't want hordes of people coming round to look at it. One of them might want to buy it."

"Well, as we discussed before, why don't you go and see about getting a mortgage? I could actually lend you quite a bit and with a decent deposit, you might manage to borrow enough to buy it."

"I can't take your money. Bless you for offering but I couldn't."

"I told you, my parents left us quite a bit. I bought my flat outright and there's still some left. I'm only lending it to you, not giving it. Go and see the bank tomorrow before we leave. See exactly what the situation is."

"I suppose I could go and talk things through with the bank. At least I'd have some idea of what I might borrow. But it would mean we'd be rather later leaving."

"Not to worry. It would be better to go

with some idea of your future rather than leave with uncertainty."

"All right. I'll phone after breakfast tomorrow and see if he can see me. If you're sure you don't mind."

"Of course not. Shall I come with you?"

"Why not? It might be good for you to hear what he says."

"What do you fancy eating? We've got various things in the fridge that need finishing. I could make something, if you like."

"Now, am I willing to risk my life that way? I'll have to think about it seriously."

"Cheek!" She laughed, punching him gently. He reached over and grabbed her hand. She hesitated and then relaxed. Gently, he tugged her closer and kissed her. She didn't resist and kissed him back. She felt her senses soaring in a totally new way... like nothing she had ever felt before and certainly never with Henry.

He let her go.

"Wow!" he exclaimed. "That was something else."

"You're right. It was magical. I've never felt like that before."

"Nor me. There must have been violins playing somewhere to accompany the feelings you provoked."

They both sat together and repeated their

kisses. It was the same magical feeling again and again.

"If we really are going to have supper, we should stop doing this, however lovely it is, and get something ready," Jed said softly.

"Spoilsport," she managed to utter. "But you're right, as always. And we don't really want anything to get out of hand, now do we?"

He said nothing but studied her hard.

"What? What are you looking at?" she demanded.

"You. Just you. You really are very beautiful – even with bits of sand still in your hair."

She laughed again and punched him gently.

"You really know how to flatter a girl, don't you?"

"Let's cook something together. That way we might both stay healthy and even enjoy supper. I think there's some wine in the fridge. You can pour some for us while we cook."

"Now that's the sort of cooking I really like."

Allergic To Marriage?

THEY made an appointment to see the bank manager at ten o'clock the next day. Jed took a collection of papers with him and fairly pessimistic hopes.

"I really don't see him going along with this," he said.

"You won't get anything from him with that attitude," Carolyn chided. "Be positive. That way he'll have to listen."

"But I really don't have much to offer as a deposit."

"I can help with that, don't forget."

"I've told you, I can't even think of accepting that. Ah well, here goes... I think it's an impossible task but I'll give it a go anyway."

They parked a little way from the bank and walked through an alleyway. It was another glorious morning. She felt almost reluctant to leave, but when she thought of the job she'd left behind or rather which had left her, she knew it was necessary.

She also thought of the previous evening and Jed's kisses. She thrilled at the thought and slipped her fingers into his free hand.

He looked at her, slightly surprised. His

warm brown eyes looked smilingly into her own dark blueish-brown ones.

"This is a new phase we're entering, isn't it?"

"I was just thinking about last evening. When you kissed me and..."

"Sorry, but we're here. This is my bank." He let her hand go and shuffled his papers in his other hand. "Here we go. Let's see what the man can offer me."

The meet and greeter lady was standing inside the doors and Jed explained the reason for their visit.

"Take a seat for a moment. I'll see is Mr Blenkinsop is ready for you," she said.

"He'll see you now," she told them a few moments later.

Jed looked rueful a little while later when they came out of his office.

"I said it wouldn't do me any good, didn't I?"

"I don't know. You can borrow about sixty percent of the amount you need. I can lend you the rest if you'll only take it."

"What I really need is to get the landlord to drop his price considerably."

"That would be good. Perhaps viewers won't offer him anything like the amount he's asking."

"Maybe. It only takes one, however. Come on. We've got a long drive ahead of us."

"I suppose so. It's so nice here, though. But I must go and see Emily. She's in a bad way, from what Sophie said. And I need to know where I'm going next. Oh, and there's a new car to buy. I'd almost forgotten about that delight."

Three hours later, they were well on their way back to Buckinghamshire. He suggested they stop for some lunch and she shrugged.

"If you like."

"The inner man requires food," he announced. "There's a service station coming up in a few miles. Glorious motorway food should fill the spot."

"Can't wait."

The journey went on and they were queuing in long traffic delays. They finally arrived at Carolyn's flat at about seven o'clock. There was a large heap of mail waiting for her and she flicked through the envelopes.

"Oh, there's something from the car insurance." She opened it and exclaimed, "That's good! They've offered me quite a large sum, more than I expected. I might even look at brand new cars."

"That sounds good. Shall we go out for something to eat? Save having to cook anything."

"I suppose we could. There's nothing

much in the freezer. Just somewhere quick. I feel worn out and you must too after driving all that way."

"I do feel weary. My brain is still humming along the motorway. Where shall we go?"

"There's a pub near the flat. Nothing special but it does reasonable food. And I want to call Emily this evening."

"Do you want to call her before we eat?"

"If you don't mind."

She dialled the number and waited. It seemed to ring forever and nobody replied.

"She must have gone out," Carolyn said. "That's encouraging, don't you think?"

"I don't know the woman. If you think it's good, it must be."

"I'll try her later. Let's go now and see what we can find to eat."

She tried Emily's number several times during the latter part of the evening and finally gave up.

"I'll make us a drink and then I think it's bedtime. I'll have to wait till tomorrow to speak to her. What do you want? Chocolate or coffee?"

"I'll go for chocolate, please. It feels strange to be a guest in your flat. It's very different to my cottage."

"Well, don't feel strange. Please, make yourself at home here."

"Thanks, I will. It's very different to my

place, though. All on one floor for starters. And it's very modern. I do like it but it seems a bit strange to me. You know, being used to older stuff."

"I love your place. This is fine for me, though. Henry said he hated it but I suspect that was because it was all mine."

"Must be the male species that has to have ownership."

They drank their chocolate and went off to their beds.

Carolyn fell asleep very quickly and woke feeling refreshed. She made tea and sat drinking it, remembering the days she had spent in Cornwall.

She'd sat out in the garden on several occasions, something she couldn't do here. Would she like to live in Cornwall? She actually thought she would. Could she live with Jed?

Yes, she decided. Yes, she could. The thought struck her. If she were to sell this flat, she could put the money towards Jed's cottage. If she were going to live there with him. Surely he couldn't object to that?

She pushed the idea to the back of her mind for the time being. She decided to call Emily again. She must be home by now, she reasoned. Again, there was no reply.

She dialled Sophie's number.

"Sophie… it's Carolyn. I've been trying to

ring Emily but can't get hold of her…"

"Oh, Carolyn, I'm so glad you've rung. I was going to call you but I didn't want to upset you while you were still in Cornwall. I knew you would be in touch as soon as you got home. Emily tried taking an overdose. Luckily, I went round to see her the same morning and found her."

"Oh, poor Emily – and poor you! That must have been quite horrible for you. Is she all right now?"

"Well, yes. But she's pretty down. I don't really think she's on top of things just yet."

"Is she still in hospital?"

"She's supposed to be coming out tomorrow."

"I'll go and see her later today then. I'm so sorry you had to go through all this. I should have been here for her."

"Don't worry about it. I'm just glad I was able to do something. She doesn't really appreciate it but there we are."

The two ex-colleagues chatted for a while longer and when she heard Jed moving around, Carolyn said she had to go. She reboiled the kettle and presented him with some tea when he appeared.

He leaned over to kiss her.

"Sleep well?"

"I did actually. Jed, something's happened. It's Emily. She tried to end her life. She's still in hospital but I really feel I need to go and see her."

"That's terrible news. Of course you must see her. But I'll drive you. You haven't got a car, remember."

"Oh, no. I must also go to the garage and see what's around."

"Let's do that this morning. And do we need some shopping?"

"The oh-so-practical Mr Jed Soames. Yes, I do need some shopping and we can go to the garage."

"I'd also like to call Paul," Jed said. "See if they're free for the evening. And I suppose I should speak to my parents. I ought to go and see them sometime."

"Yes, of course. Where do they live?"

"Out towards Rugby. It's quite a longish way so I'd need to go for a whole day."

"You go off whenever you like. I can always hire a car to run around in."

"Maybe tomorrow, then? I'll call them later and see if they're around. You could always come with me?"

"I think you ought to go on your own, actually. You can tell them about me if you want to."

"Really? That sounds almost promising."

"Maybe," she said with a smile. "You simply never know what will happen, do you?"

They went to the garage first and looked at several new models. She had decided to look for a similar one to the one that had been stolen and burned but the garage didn't have any available. They went to another garage and found something similar.

"You could have it in a couple of weeks," the salesman told her.

"But I need it much sooner than that. Have you got something I could borrow?" She also told him her saga about having her car stolen.

"I'm sure we can do something. Your insurance will pay, won't they?"

By the time they had finished negotiating, she had a nice little red car to drive away and the order was placed for her new one. They left one very happy salesman behind them.

"Do you want to go back to the flat? I can always do the shopping on my own."

"What, and deprive me of the total pleasure of the supermarket visit? Certainly not. I wouldn't miss it for the world. You lead the way in your new hire car and I'll follow."

They set off together along the road and she parked some distance from the crowded shop. Jed joined her and they had soon filled the trolley.

"I ought to get something to take to Emily. What do you think? Some flowers perhaps?"

"I've no idea. Does she like flowers?"

"I suppose so." They added a bunch and went to pay. "My bill this time. You're my guest, so no arguments."

"Very well. I wouldn't dream of intruding on your shopping habits." They drove back to the flat and took in the shopping.

"Maybe I'll go out with my camera this afternoon. Leave you to go to the hospital on your own. Now you're an independent driver again."

"Fine. There some nice walks around."

"I have been here before, remember. I lived here for quite a while."

"Sorry. I think of you as living in Cornwall. Hard to realise you once were a city boy."

"That's now way into my past. I'm glad to say, my business is starting to take off. And it's something I love doing."

"You do it well, too. Right. I'll make us a sandwich for now, if that's OK."

It seemed strange to be on her own for the first time in a while. She drove to the hospital and asked at the desk which ward Emily was in.

She felt totally shocked when she saw her friend and former boss. Emily looked emaciated and somehow shrunken.

Carolyn fixed a smile on her face and spoke to her as normally as she was able.

"I do hope you're feeling better, Emily. I've brought you some flowers. Sorry I wasn't able to come earlier but I'm only just back from Cornwall." Then she ran out of anything to say.

"I am sorry, my dear. It seemed the only way out. I do feel foolish. Couldn't even do this one thing satisfactorily."

"You must have felt desperate. I must admit, I was pretty low myself when... well, when Henry ran out on me."

"You seem to have got over that all right. I must say, you look better than I've seen you in ages."

"I am. But how about you? How do you feel now?"

"Foolish, as I said. The fire, well it was all my fault. I must have left something on when I left the night before. It seems it was an electric failing due to something overheating."

"I don't see why you should think it's your fault. It could have been any of us who left something on."

"No, dear. I know it was me."

"You mean you left something on, on purpose?"

She looked away from Carolyn.

"Things weren't going so well lately. But

don't tell anyone I said that. I don't want to get anyone into trouble."

"I won't say anything. But you always seemed to be on top of everything. Orders were always there. I never realised anything was wrong."

"Nothing is quite as it seems. Now, tell me about your stay in Cornwall. It's a lovely part of the world, isn't it?"

For the next few minutes Carolyn talked of the lovely places she'd seen and the cottage, Jed's cottage.

"And this Jed. Is he the new man in your life?"

"I think he may be. I did see Henry while I was there. He's working in a shop. Strange but he said he's enjoying it."

"That doesn't sound like your Henry."

"He isn't my Henry. Not at all."

"I'm glad to hear it. I never felt he was right for you. Always seemed a bit well, sly, I suppose."

"Goodness. You never intimated you didn't like him."

"I'll never forget the look on your face when you ran into the church that day. You looked like a she-devil!"

She smiled.

"I wouldn't have liked to be on the receiving end of it when you found him."

"Well, lucky for him I didn't find him.

Well, not that day at any rate."

"You know something, my dear, I feel much better for having talked to you."

"You look better. Much more alive. I felt worried when I came in and saw you lying there."

"The insurance will pay me something for the business. I might just retire now. Start doing things I never had time for. I do feel bad about my staff, though. Perhaps they'll give me enough to allow me to pay them something."

"Don't worry about it. They'll all get jobs soon enough. I know Sophie has got a new job already."

"We'll see. I'm going home tomorrow. They say I should be all right to go anyway."

"I'll come and fetch you if you like."

"Don't worry. I can get a taxi. Or maybe they'll send me home in one of their vehicles."

"Nonsense. What time are you due to be discharged?"

"After lunch. I have to see the psychiatrist before I go. To check me out."

"Right. So if I come about the same time as today?"

"Well, thank you very much. If you're sure."

The arrangements were made. Carolyn would buy a few basics for Emily to see her home and whatever Jed was doing, he'd have to do it on his own.

This was important to her and she wanted to know she'd done her best for her old boss.

****

"So, it looks as though I'm in the job market again," she told Jed over supper. "Emily is thinking of taking early retirement and we're all, her staff that is, now free."

"My offer of working with me in some sort of shop is still open. I think it might be rather nice to work together. You could soon learn to help me, too. Seeing how well you worked when we were doing the brochures for Mrs James."

"I didn't do much. But I don't know. Working in a shop all day doesn't really appeal much. Besides, it would mean I'd have to move to Cornwall."

"Would that be so hard?"

"I don't know. Maybe not. I do love it there. Actually, I was thinking. If I sell this place, maybe you'd accept the money towards buying your cottage. It would mean, of course, that I'd have to come and live with you."

He stared at her, almost disbelieving what he was hearing.

"Do you mean that? Really?"

She burst out laughing.

"Of course I do. I love you, Jed. Don't look quite so amazed. You're a very loveable guy. But there's just one thing. I want us to wait till we're married. You know what I mean. Wait, I've just remembered, you told me when we first met, you're allergic to marriage."

"That was after Gemma left me in the lurch. Besides, at the time, I thought you were pretty against marriage yourself."

"That was because of Henry, of course. I was a bit sensitive at that time. In fact, the day Paul introduced us, it was my first outing as a single woman."

"Well, you managed it all very well. See? I fell in love with you right away. We need to go out to celebrate. I'll call Paul and Mel. They can join us tomorrow night. We'll have us a banquet."

"I'm going to collect Emily from hospital tomorrow afternoon, actually. Hope you don't mind. I wondered if you might go to see your parents?"

"I shall postpone that trip till you have time to come, too. Now we're planning to live together, they'll need to see you. By the way, I haven't actually asked you to marry me."

"I suppose not. I assumed you do want to

marry me…"

"I do believe you asked me first? I will consider it carefully and let you know."

She looked at him somewhat shocked but said nothing. Maybe he really was allergic to marriage.

The subject seemed to have been dropped for the rest of the evening. So much for her making assumptions. She knew she really ought to say something to him but she couldn't.

"Shall I call Paul and invite him out tomorrow?" she said at last.

"I'll call him if you like."

"As you like. It's number one on the phone."

"Cheers." Jed pressed the speed dial button.

Carolyn listened to what he said as he spoke to her brother. She was expecting he would tell Paul about them being engaged but he said nothing.

She felt ridiculously hurt. It was all rather silly, she was thinking. She had assumed it was all go ahead and arrange the wedding but Jed hadn't reacted in the way she had expected. Granted, at first he'd seemed excited and there had been talk of a banquet. But now, he hadn't said anything to her brother.

"So, we'll see you tomorrow evening

then?" Jed said as he finished the call. "Oh, Carolyn sends her love, by the way." He hung up.

"I'd have liked a word or two actually," she told him.

"Sorry. I wasn't thinking. Never mind, we'll see them tomorrow. You can have all the words you want then. Now, I'm going to wash up and then turn in. Is that all right with you?"

"I can do the clearing. You go to bed, if you're tired."

"I'll do it first. You can dry and put away."

She watched Jed as he efficiently finished the washing up and left everywhere very tidy. He went up to bed and she followed a short while later, her thoughts running round in small circles.

Had she misinterpreted what he felt about her?

Celebrations!

THE next day, clutching his cameras, Jed went off on his own to photograph various local scenes. He said nothing about marriage or weddings and she certainly didn't want to raise the subject again.

Carolyn had to admit, she felt rather hurt by his reaction. Instead, she went to collect her friend Emily from the hospital. She had called at the stores first to buy bread and milk and one or two treats for her friend and ex-boss.

She went to the ward and saw Emily was ready to go, her little suitcase packed and ready by the bed.

"This is very good of you, Carolyn," Emily said. "I do appreciate it."

"No problem. Looks as if you're all set to go?"

"Yes, I am. Glad to get out of this place, actually. The nurses are very kind but I'm looking forward to going home."

"Well, as long as you're sure you're ready..." Caroline remarked.

"Oh, don't worry. I wouldn't try it again. I realise now how silly it was. And you know, I'm never going to drink again. I drank nearly a half a bottle of something or other. I scarcely knew what I was doing."

"Wow, that is dangerous! Alcohol can be really depressing."

"Especially if you're not used to it. I guess I learned my lesson. You know, I'm really glad I was unsuccessful. Life is certainly not all that bad."

"I'm glad to hear you say so."

They walked down the stairs and out to Carolyn's car.

"Oh, you've changed your car. How long have you had this one?"

"It's a hired one. I've ordered a new one but it will take a while to get to me. I'll put your case in the back."

It took only minutes to drive to Emily's home. She wished she'd thought of going there before delivering Emily back, if only to put flowers in and air it.

They went inside and Emily gasped in surprise. There were several lots of flowers and everywhere was sparkling clean. There were even supplies in the fridge, making Carolyn's purchases redundant.

"Oh, my goodness! Who has done all this?" Emily said, quite overwhelmed.

"There's a card on the shelf. Open it and see what it says."

"Oh, how lovely," Emily said when she opened the card. "The girls from the office

have done it all. I gave Sophie my keys
when she offered to pick up my mail and
bring it to the hospital. The card says,
'Wishing you a speedy return to your usual
excellent health. With Love from Sophie,
Annabel and Mary'. Isn't that nice?"

"Lovely. Look, I've got you a few bits and
pieces to start you off again. I'll put them in
the fridge anyway. Would you like a cup of
tea?"

"That would be lovely, dear. Thank you
very much. But I can do it, you know."

"Of course you can, but make the most of
me. I somehow don't think I'm going to be
around all that much longer. I'm thinking of
moving to Cornwall."

"Cornwall? Why ever are you going
there? I thought it was just a holiday place."

"People live there, too, you know."

"Oh, is this something to do with the
young man you met?"

"Jed. Yes."

"Jed's a funny name. What's it short for?"

"I've no idea. I assumed he was just called
Jed. I'll have to ask him."

They drank their tea and at last, Carolyn
said it was time she was leaving.

"I'll call you in the morning. Make sure
you have everything you'll need."

"Thank you very much. But you've no
need to worry. I've got food in the freezer

and my car's in the garage. I'm going to begin my new life tomorrow."

"OK, then. You look after yourself. I'll still call tomorrow anyway," Carolyn promised.

"'Bye now, love. And I hope you'll be very happy with your new man."

Carolyn drove home and looked for Jed's car. It wasn't parked outside. She shrugged and went back inside her flat. It was undisturbed and looked just as she had left it. Whatever he was doing, Jed hadn't returned since she left.

She went into her room to try to decide what to wear that evening. She felt it might be quite an occasion and didn't want to look anything less than smart. Mel always looked good and Carolyn didn't want to let anyone down.

She tried on several outfits before deciding on a short black cocktail type of dress. Then she sighed, remembering it was the one she had worn for her engagement party. It most certainly wouldn't do for this evening.

She really needed something different. She remembered some of the new things she had bought for their honeymoon. She foraged in the wardrobe and came out with a deep blue silky dress. It was strapless and hopefully, would be ideal.

She tried it on and pirouetted in front of the mirror. This was the one. Never worn before, it seemed perfect.

"Anyone at home?" Jed called.

"Just coming," she called back, quickly stripping off the dress and pulling on her jeans again.

"How did you get on?" she asked.

"Fine. How was Emily?"

"She seemed OK, thankfully. Said she'd got herself drunk before she took the pills and didn't really know what she was doing. Promised me she'd never try it again, anyway."

"And you believed her?"

"Yes. I really think she meant it. So, have you decided where we're going this evening?"

"I thought the pub near here. Paul and Mel will come here first and they'll give us a lift."

"Oh, I see." Her blue dress was much too smart for the pub. She felt slightly disappointed. "I'd better go and choose something to wear," she said.

"Make it something smart," Jed suggested.

"Not too smart for that pub. I'd get drummed out for exposing too much flesh." She laughed.

"Why? What were you thinking of wearing?"

"Oh, just a sun dress. But there's plenty of

choice there. I'll maybe go for some fairly new jeans."

"The sun dress sounds nice. Wear that."

"Bit dressy for the pub." She didn't notice the twinkle in his eye as she continued to argue.

"I'm going to wear my new suit and I've even bought a tie."

"New suit? And a tie? Isn't that a bit much, for you, I mean?"

"Only the best for my lady."

"Where are we really going? It isn't the pub, is it?"

"No. You're all too easy to tease. We have a table booked at The Pink Pelican. Very exclusive, don't you know. Ties are always worn as a matter of course."

He spoke in such a silly posh voice, she soon collapsed into laughter.

"That sounds lovely. Wonderful, in fact. Thank you. Do Paul and Mel know we're going there?"

"They do indeed. They offered to collect us so we don't have to worry about driving. Is that agreeable to you, madame?"

"Sounds wonderful. But won't they want to have a drink?"

"Evidently Mel's flying off in the morning so she'll be driving early. I shall now go and change. That's where I was this afternoon by the way. Buying my new suit."

"I see. And what time are we going out?"

"Seven o'clock they're coming here."

"Then I'd better go and start getting ready, hadn't I?"

"You had indeed. I could do with a shower. I got very warm in the shops in and out of different clothes. Could have done with you there to help me but I hope you like it."

"I'm sure I shall. Go on then, go and shower. I'll go in after you."

She heard him singing as he showered. He had a surprisingly good voice, she remembered from their evening of folk singing. He sounded happy and she smiled with pleasure.

She changed into the blue dress and fixed a narrow gold chain round her neck. She couldn't decide what to do with her hair. It looked much lighter than before her holiday in Cornwall and she quite liked it. She brushed it and left it loose. A quick touch of lip gloss and she felt as if she was ready.

She went downstairs and saw Jed, standing in the lounge, holding a glass of champagne.

"Goodness me," she said.

"I wanted to start the evening well," Jed told her.

"Well, it looks as if you've scored highly all ready. And I love the suit. And the tie is also perfect. Exactly what I'd have chosen."

"I'm glad."

So what exactly are we celebrating?"
Carolyn asked him.

"Nothing really. I just fancied treating us
to something pleasant to drink."

"Oh, I see." She tried to hide her
disappointment.

"Paul and Mel will be here soon. It's
almost seven. I'll save some champers to
give to them."

"Not to Mel, though."

"She'll have one small glass, I'm sure. You
ready for a top up?"

"I'll be tipsy before we get too much
further..."

"Then I'd better ask you before you do.
Carolyn, will you marry me?" He even went
down on one knee as he spoke.

"I will."

Her eyes filled with tears and she held out
her hand to him.

He got up and said, "I hope you like this
ring. If you don't I've kept the bill and we
can go and change it tomorrow."

From his pocket he took out a small box
and opened it. He held out a ring she
absolutely fell in love with on first sight.

"Oh, it's lovely. I love it." He slipped it on
to her finger and it was a perfect fit. "Oh,
thank you. Thank you so much."

"Good. I took a bit of a risk but glad you like it."

"How did you know what size to get?"

"I'm afraid I was a bit naughty. I looked in your dressing table drawer and found the old one. Henry's ring, I suppose it was. I borrowed it and took it with me to the jewellers. Hope you don't mind."

"I think that was pretty ingenious of you. Well done."

"Here's the old one back. You might want to put it back in your dressing-table."

"Must admit, I'd quite forgotten it was there. I'll give it back to Henry at some point. I love the ring you chose. Thank you."

"I'm glad. I think Paul and Mel should be here anytime. They don't know anything about our plans yet so it will be a surprise to them."

"I think Paul will be slightly shocked actually."

"Maybe. I doubt it though. He realised my intentions from the start."

The doorbell rang.

"I'll let them in, shall I?" Jed offered.

"Please. Gosh, what a day this is turning out to be."

Jed was nearly bursting with his news as he ushered Paul and Mel into the room.

"We've got something to tell you. We're

engaged! Have some champagne to help us celebrate."

"Well done, sis!" Paul was evidently delighted. "I'm so pleased. Congratulations to both of you."

He raised the glass Jed handed to him.

"Yes, congratulations!" Mel added. "When's the big day?"

"Nothing planned yet. It's only just happened."

"But you've got a ring already?" Mel asked.

"Yes, isn't it gorgeous?" Carolyn held out her hand for inspection.

"Very elegant. It suits you. Much better than the other one. Whoops, shouldn't have said that..."

"It's OK. I know it's a much nicer one than the one Henry gave me. I saw him recently. He's living about five miles away from Jed. Working in a shop, would you believe?"

"Nothing surprises me about him. Anyway," Paul said, raising his glass again, "here's to you both. May you be happy and enjoy your lives together. Actually, we're planning to get married pretty soon, too."

"Well, congratulations! About time, I should say. You two have been together for years!" Jed smiled.

"Years and years," Mel agreed. "I'm getting a new job. Just short runs to the

Continent and back in the same day. It'll make such a difference to us."

"Looks like we'll all be making huge changes to our lives. Perhaps we should consider a joint wedding. Save on the cost of it all," Carolyn joked.

"Well actually, we're just planning a small do at the local registry office. Just one or two friends and a meal afterwards. Hope you'll be able to be there."

"Try stopping us," Carolyn said.

"It's next weekend," Paul told them.

"Next weekend? You don't waste time, do you, mate?" Jed remarked.

"No point. It's about time I made an honest woman of her." Paul ducked to avoid the inevitable playful punch from Mel.

"Hey, you," she retorted, "just watch what you're saying."

"It's maybe a bit soon for us. We'll have our wedding pretty soon, though, won't we, darling?" Jed said.

"I suppose so. Not at the weekend, though. Wow, we really have something to celebrate, don't we?"

"Certainly do. Let's get this show on the road," Jed said, and they all trooped out to the car.

It was a perfect evening and when they all went back to Carolyn's flat, they were still in great spirits. Suddenly, Caroline spoke.

"Tell me something, Jed. What's Jed short for? I can't believe you were really baptised with that as a name."

"You don't want to know."

"I do. Come on. Do you know, Paul?"

"I've no idea."

Jed closed his eyes.

"You'll never believe it."

"Come on, then." They were all listening avidly.

"It's Jermyn Daniel. JD or Jed for short. The only people in the world who call me Jermyn are my parents. Now do you see why I was hesitant about taking you to see them?"

"What on earth is wrong with that as a name?"

"It's so, well, unheard of. Anyway, forget I told you. I don't want ever to hear it from any of you again."

"No problem, Jermyn. We'll forget it immediately, if not sooner," Paul teased. "Come on, love, we'd better go if you're to get your flight in the morning."

They said goodnight and went off.

"Now if I'm coming to Cornwall to live with you, please won't you accept some money from me? I can't bear to live anywhere but in your cottage."

"I don't like to," he repeated.

"I'm going to put this place on the market

and if you don't accept my money, then I shall be the first person to bid for your cottage when it goes on the market."

"In that case, thank you very much. I'll phone the landlord in the morning and make him an offer."

"Good. I think that concludes the business for today." She giggled.

"Except to tell you I love you, Carolyn Brown."

"And I love you, Jermyn Soames."

The End.

Published in Great Britain by D.C. Thomson & Co., Ltd., Dundee, Glasgow and London. Distributed by Marketforce, Blue Fin Building, 110 Southwark Street, London SE1 0SU.
Tel: +44 (0) 20 3148 3300. Fax: +44 (0) 20 3148 8105.
Website: www.marketforce.co.uk
© D.C. Thomson & Co., Ltd., and Chrissie Loveday, 2014

Don't miss the next Pocket Novel No. 772,
On sale December 18, 2014.

If you are looking for back numbers please telephone 0800 318846
Printed and bound by CPI Group (UK) Ltd., Croydon, CR0 4YY